JOLINE I

Before I Go

For those in need of self-kindness,
where forgiveness extends not only to others
but to the echoes within ourselves.

This story explores themes of grief, loss, and healing. It delves into the emotional complexities of navigating tragedy and the process of forgiveness, touching the sensitive aspects of mourning a loved one. Reader discretion is advised for those who may find these themes challenging or triggering.

Contents

Acknowledgement

To my mom, Chat, my dad, Joseph, and brother, Joshua, your unwavering support during my late-night reading and writing escapades, along with your gentle reminders to get some sleep past 3 in the morning, mean the world to me.

To 8Letters Bookstore and Publishing, thank you for being involved and instrumental in turning my dream into reality.

And to my treasured readers, your journey with Rory and Walker is a gift. May you discover light, hope and forgiveness within my written pages. Thank you for embracing my book! This isn't the end.

I hope you'll join me in the stories to come.

1

A Letter to Harper

Dear Harper,

  It's been a year since you left us, and not a single day has passed without the echo of your absence reverberating through our lives. As I sit here, penning down my thoughts, it feels like I'm reaching out to a world where you're still present, where your laughter dances in the air, and your advice guides me through life.

The pain is still fresh, Harper, as if time has chosen to stand still in the void you left behind. I find myself caught between the moments we shared and the future that now stretches out without you. The car accident, like a cruel twist of fate, snatched you away from us, leaving our family shattered and my heart irreparably broken.

I miss you in the quiet moments, Harper—when the world is hushed, and the only sound is the beating of my own heart, a heartbeat that echoes with the memory of yours. Your absence is a silent scream in the stillness of the night, and your laughter, once so vivid, now feels like a distant melody fading into the shadows.

There's a peculiar ache that accompanies the passage of time without you. It's a paradox, Harper, because while the days continue to unfold, it's as if I'm trapped in a never-ending moment of grief. I long to hear your voice, to share my victories and defeats, and to seek the comfort only a big brother can provide.

Time may have softened the edges of others' pain, but it has not dulled the ache within my soul. I'm learning to navigate this world without you, Harper, but the path is strewn with the fragments of a life that once was whole.

As the seasons change, I find myself clinging to the memories we made—the laughter, the arguments, the shared secrets. Your absence is a void that no amount of time can fill. I ache for the conversations we'll never have, the milestones you'll never witness, and the simple joy of having you by my side.

Harper, my heart still breaks for you. You were more than a brother; you were my confidant, my ally, and my friend. Life without you is like a puzzle missing a crucial piece—incomplete and forever yearning for what once was.

So, I write this letter to you, Harper, not as a farewell but as an eternal connection. In the symphony of life, your melody lingers, and though I may not hear it with my ears, I feel it in the depths of my soul. Until we meet again in the realms beyond, know that you are loved, missed, and cherished every single day.

With love that transcends time,
  Rory

2

The Lake

The sun dipped below the horizon, casting long shadows that stretched across the empty rooms of our once vibrant house. Summer had arrived, bringing with it the haunting echo of memories and the weight of solitude. For the umpteenth time, my parents had left town, escaping the suffocating atmosphere that lingered in the air since Harper's departure. As the front door clicked shut, the hollowness of the house enveloped me, and I found myself navigating the quiet corridors alone.

This had become the routine ever since that fateful day, the day Harper left us. Each summer, my parents sought refuge elsewhere, leaving me to grapple with the ghosts that clung to the walls like shadows. The reasons they gave were varied—work, a change of scenery, the need to "get away." But in the depths of my heart, I couldn't help but feel that it was an escape from me, from the lingering guilt that seemed to have settled like a heavy fog in our home.

The rooms echoed with silence, a stark contrast to the laughter that used to resound through the walls when Harper was alive. I wandered through the house, feeling the emptiness seeping into my bones. In the kitchen, I stared at the empty chairs around the dining table, where family dinners had once been a cherished ritual. Now, the chairs stood as silent witnesses to a void that no amount of absence could fill.

I climbed the creaky stairs, passing by Harper's room—a sacred space frozen in time. The door remained closed, a barricade against the pain that lurked within. I couldn't bring myself to enter, fearing that the weight of his absence would crush me once more. Instead, I sought refuge in my own room, a sanctuary of solitude where I could confront the demons that haunted my thoughts.

As the sun painted the sky with hues of orange and pink, I found myself on the rooftop, gazing at the stars that had witnessed our shared dreams. The summer breeze whispered through the empty spaces, carrying with it a sense of longing. I couldn't escape the feeling that my parents' absence was more than just a physical departure—it was a silent accusation, an unspoken blame.

The night stretched before me like an endless canvas of loneliness. I lay on the roof, tracing constellations with my eyes, each star a distant memory of a brother I could no longer touch. The weight of isolation pressed down on me, and I wondered if my parents saw me as a living reminder of the tragedy that had befallen our family.

In the depths of the night, I whispered words to the wind, hoping they would reach Harper wherever he was.

"I miss you," I confessed to the vast expanse of darkness. "And I'm sorry if I'm the reason they had to leave." The stars remained silent witnesses to my soliloquy, and the shadows continued to dance around me.

Alone in the silence of our empty house, I yearned for a connection that surpassed the boundaries of this world. The summer stretched ahead, a solitary journey through the corridors of loss, and I clung to the hope that, one day, the echoes of our shared laughter would drown out the haunting silence that surrounded me.

* * *

The decision to step out into the sun the next day felt foreign, a hesitant rebellion against the suffocating solitude within our house. The sunlight, though warm, cast long shadows on the uneven pavement as I strolled down the familiar streets. At sixteen, I found myself navigating a world that seemed both indifferent and unfamiliar. Harper had been my anchor, my guide through the intricacies of life, but now I was adrift, clinging to memories like a sailor to a lifebuoy in a storm.

The lake, hidden deep within the forest, beckoned like an old friend. Harper and I had discovered it years ago, a secluded sanctuary where the world melted away, leaving only the rhythmic lull of water and the rustle of leaves as company. Today, I decided to revisit that sacred place, hoping the echoes of our laughter would resurface amidst the tranquility of nature.

As I packed a simple bag, memories of past summers flooded my mind. Harper, with his easy charm, had been the social butterfly—the MVP, the eloquent speaker, the golden boy. I, on the other hand, found solace in the pages of books and sought refuge in the quiet corners of the library. We were an odd pair, but he was the only friend I needed, the one who embraced my quirks and made the world seem less daunting.

The forest welcomed me with a symphony of chirping birds

and the crunch of leaves beneath my worn-out sneakers. The sunlight filtered through the foliage, casting dappled patterns on the path ahead. With each step, the weight on my shoulders seemed to lift, replaced by a tentative sense of freedom.

The lake emerged; a serene expanse framed by the lush embrace of trees. The memories of laughter and shared secrets enveloped me, like whispers carried by the gentle breeze. I stripped down to my swimsuit, a simple act that felt like shedding layers of grief, and waded into the cool embrace of the water.

The lake, once a place of solace, now mirrored the ache in my heart. The rhythmic clapping of the waves seemed to synchronize with the pulsating pain within me. I swam aimlessly, each stroke a futile attempt to escape the currents of grief that threatened to pull me under.

As the sun dipped lower, casting a warm glow across the water, I felt the heaviness intensify. The question lingered in my mind like a haunting refrain: What if I just let go? The lake seemed like a silent accomplice to my contemplation, its depths holding the secrets of countless stories.

Without conscious thought, I surrendered to the water, letting it engulf me. The world beneath the surface was a quiet realm, a surreal ballet of shadows and light. The ache in my chest mirrored the pressure in my ears as I sank deeper into the abyss.

Just as the edges of consciousness began to blur, a firm grip closed around my hand, yanking me upward. Gasping for air, I found myself back at the surface, reality crashing back with each desperate breath. The savior, a stranger with concerned eyes, anchored me to the present.

"What were you thinking?" he asked, his voice a mixture of

disbelief and concern.

I could only manage a shaky exhale, my heart pounding in my ears. In that moment, I realized the depth of my despair, the dangerous allure of surrender. As the stranger's eyes held mine, I saw a reflection of the questions that haunted me – would someone miss me? Would someone care?

For now, in the embrace of a stranger beneath the fading sunlight, I clung to the fragile thread connecting me to the world above the surface.

3

The Stranger

The stranger's hazel eyes met mine, concern etched across his beautiful face. He looked as young as I was, with curly hair that danced in the wind, a face that held an air of kindness, and eyes that mirrored genuine worry. Shame flooded my senses, realizing that someone had witnessed a vulnerable moment, a glimpse into the depths of my struggle.

"I'm sorry," I stammered, my voice barely audible above the residual echoes of the lake.

His response was gentle, a reassuring smile accompanying his outstretched hand. "No need to be sorry. I'm Walker," he said, his words a lifeline in the aftermath of a silent battle.

I took his hand in mine. "I'm Rory," I responded with a tight smile.

We stood there, the sun casting long shadows as the lake cradled our secrets. Walker and I began to converse, the weight of our encounter lifting with each shared word. He confessed that today marked his first discovery of the lake, and his initial joy had turned to sheer panic upon seeing someone struggling in the water.

We laughed it off, the tension unraveling in the shared warmth of amusement. For the first time in ages, I felt lighter. Walker's kindness, his willingness to laugh with me, provided a respite from the constant ache that clung to me like a persistent shadow.

As we sat on the lake's edge, the conversation shifted. Walker's hazel eyes held a genuine curiosity as he asked about my connection to the lake. I hesitated, the memories of Harper dancing on the edges of my consciousness. Finally, I mustered the courage to share.

"This was my brother's favorite lake," I admitted, my voice tinged with both nostalgia and sorrow.

A sympathetic nod was Walker's only response, no probing questions or intrusive curiosity. It was a relief. He respected the boundaries of my grief, and in that unspoken understanding, I found solace.

"Where is he now?" Walker inquired; his question laced with gentle concern.

The answer hovered between truth and evasion. "Far away," I replied, a vague response that left the details shrouded in ambiguity.

The fading sunlight reminded us that it was time to leave. The lake, once a place of solace and struggle, had become a stage for a newfound connection. As we walked away from the water's edge, Walker turned to me with a question that echoed in the quiet space between us.

"Will I be seeing you again?"

The pulse in my veins quickened, a mixture of surprise and anticipation. It was a question that held the promise of something beyond the fleeting encounter at the lake. I hesitated for a moment, then nodded, a genuine smile playing on my lips.

"Yeah, Walker. I think you will."

In that simple exchange, beneath the fading daylight, I discovered a spark of hope—a possibility of connection in a world that had felt desolate for far too long. As we parted ways, the echoes of laughter and shared secrets lingered, and I couldn't help but feel grateful that, for the first time since Harper's departure, someone had entered my world and brought a sliver of light into the shadows.

4

Alone

The door creaked open, and I stepped into the house that had become both a sanctuary and a silent witness to my solitude. The emptiness within these walls felt less oppressive tonight, as if the presence of a stranger by the lake had cast a subtle spell, dispelling the shadows that clung to me.

For the first time, the silence didn't seem to stretch endlessly before me. I moved through the familiar spaces, feeling a newfound lightness. The echoes of my footsteps reverberated, filling the void with a semblance of company. The kitchen, once a place of functional necessity, became a canvas for a culinary experiment.

I took out a frozen lasagna from the supermarket, something I bought on impulse during one of my rare ventures outside. As I preheated the oven, the simple act of preparing dinner took on significance beyond sustenance. The aroma of cooking filled the air, a comforting reminder that life persisted even in the midst of loss.

As I set the table for one, a strange sense of accomplishment washed over me. The lasagna, when it emerged golden and bubbling from the oven, felt like a triumph. I savored each bite, the flavors melding in my mouth like a symphony of tastes. In that moment, the act of dining alone transformed into a celebration of newfound resilience.

The solitude, instead of pressing down on me like a weight, felt like a choice. For the first time, I wasn't lonely. The emptiness was still there, but tonight it seemed to coexist with a newfound sense of acceptance. The lake, Walker, the shared laughter – they had become beacons of connection, lighting up the corners of my world that had long been shrouded in darkness.

As I washed the dishes, my thoughts drifted back to Walker. Was he new in town? Did he just move here? His face, with those hazel eyes and that easy smile, was etched into my memory. I wondered about the stories he carried, the reasons that brought him to our quiet corner of the world.

The evening unfolded with quiet contentment. I curled up on the couch, a book in hand, the familiar pages offering solace. The house, once a haunting echo of loss, now held the resonance of shared laughter and the promise of new connections.

In the quiet moments before sleep claimed me, I couldn't help but feel a spark of anticipation. The question lingered in the shadows of my thoughts – would I see Walker again? The possibility felt like a gentle breeze, stirring the stillness of my existence. For the first time in a long while, my heart held a glimmer of hope that went beyond the pages of memories.

The soft chime of my phone interrupted the quietude of the house. I glanced at the screen, and the familiar caller ID revealed my father's name. Picking up, I pressed the phone to my ear, the sound of his voice a distant echo through the receiver.

"Hey, Dad," I greeted, my tone carrying a mix of familiarity and detachment.

"Rory, sweetheart," his voice crackled, a product of the miles between us. "Just a quick call. We'll be extending our stay for a bit longer. Work-related stuff, you know how it is."

I sighed, a rehearsed response that held both acceptance and a subtle resignation. "No worries, Dad. I understand."

He continued, "We wired some money to your account for your personal expenses. Make sure you take care of yourself, okay?"

The routine nature of our conversation played out, each word a well-practiced script. I assured him that I would manage, that the money was appreciated, that I understood the demands of their work and that I didn't need him to send someone to check up on me. The call ended as abruptly as it began, leaving me with the distant hum of the dial tone.

As I set the phone down, the emptiness of the house closed in on me once more. It wasn't the first time they had prolonged their stay, and it wouldn't be the last. Work, their escape from the pervasive grief that lingered within our walls, became the rationale for their distance. I couldn't blame them, not really. After all, I was the reason Harper got into that car that night.

Closing my eyes, I willed away the painful memories that threatened to resurface. Not now, I told myself. Not tonight. The weight of guilt, a burden I carried since Harper's departure, pressed against my chest. I pushed it aside, burying it deep within the recesses of my thoughts.

The house, with its silent corridors and empty rooms, became both a haven and a prison. In the stillness, I grappled with the choices that led us to this fractured existence. The memories of Harper, the guilt, the loneliness—they formed a tapestry that clung to the very fabric of my being.

In the solitude that followed the call, I found solace in the routine. I cleaned up the remnants of dinner, washed the dishes, and tidied the spaces that seemed to yearn for a semblance of order. The money wired to my account served as a lifeline, a reminder that, even from a distance, my parents sought to ease the burden of my existence.

As I settled into bed, I acknowledged the silent whispers that lingered in the shadows. Harper's absence, the strained connections with my parents, the weight of guilt—they were the ghosts that danced in the periphery of my thoughts. But tonight, I chose to push them away, to seek refuge in the sanctuary of a newfound connection by the lake.

In the darkness, I whispered a promise to myself—to face the memories when the time was right, to navigate the labyrinth of grief on my terms. For now, the night held the echoes of distance, the soft murmur of solitude, and the promise of a new dawn.

5

Dream Within a Dream

The room shimmered the soft glow of moonlight, casting ethereal shadows on the familiar surroundings. In the realm of dreams, I found myself transported back to a moment suspended in time—my 10th birthday. Harper, a fourteen-year-old magician of surprises, had tiptoed into my room at the stroke of midnight.

A single cupcake, adorned with a flickering candle, was cradled in his hands. Harper's voice, a gentle whisper-sing, roused me from sleep. "Happy birthday, cupcake," he greeted, the words wrapped in the warmth of sibling affection.

I smiled at him, a mixture of surprise and delight. Harper was always full of unexpected gestures, and at midnight, he became the orchestrator of a birthday serenade. We sat on the edge of my bed, bathed in the soft glow of the candle, and talked about dreams that seemed as infinite as the night sky.

"What's your birthday wish, Rory?" Harper asked, his eyes holding a knowing twinkle.

I pondered for a moment; my gaze fixed on the dancing flame.

"I wish for time to skip, to fast forward to the good parts. I want to travel the world, Harper."

He laughed, the sound of a melody that vibrated through the room. "You will, cupcake. I promise you that. One day, you'll explore every corner of this world."

Then, the scene shifted.

I was fifteen, and the sunlit room held the promise of infinite possibilities.

The door burst open, and there he was—my brother Harper, the orchestrator of joy. With a goofy grin on his face, he embarked on a mission to serenade me with the off-key rendition of "Fifteen" by Taylor Swift. His voice wavered, notes eluding him like fireflies dancing just out of reach.

"This is life before you know who you're gonna be... at fifteen!" he belted out, the pitch defiantly off-kilter. It was a comical symphony, a performance only Harper could pull off, and I couldn't help but dissolve into laughter.

"Oh, Harper," I chuckled, the sound echoing through the dream. "You might want to steer clear of the singing path. I love you but it's not for you."

He winked at me, the mischievous glint in his eyes untouched by the lack of vocal prowess. "Who knows? I might be the next Harry Styles."

"Oh, please, don't."

"That's what makes you beautiful!" Harper's musical mishap became a cherished melody, a reminder that perfection wasn't a prerequisite for happiness. And as I woke, the echoes of laughter lingered, a sweet refrain of a dream within a dream.

The tears that stung my eyes were a bittersweet testament to the beauty of moments forever frozen in time. The weight of Harper's absence pressed against my chest, and I knew that the dreamscape held both solace and ache.

I descended the stairs, the silence of the house amplifying the echoes of memories. Determined to reclaim a fragment of that cherished memory, I searched for a cupcake in the kitchen, those cheap ones you can buy in grocery stores. Finding one, I delicately placed a single candle on its crown. The flickering flame mirrored the dance of the past, a bridge between then and now.

"Happy 17th birthday, Rory," I whispered to myself, the words a delicate promise to the girl who once wished for time to fast forward. Closing my eyes, I made a wish, not for grand adventures or worldly treasures, but for everything to be okay again—a plea for the fractured pieces of my world to find a way to mend.

In the soft glow of the candlelight, I blew out the flame, a silent offering to the universe. The room embraced the stillness, and for a fleeting moment, I felt a connection to the brother who had made midnight wishes a timeless tradition.

6

The Library

The public library stood just a few blocks from my house, a sanctuary of stories that had been a second home for as long as I could remember. Today marked the beginning of a new chapter as I stepped through its familiar doors, not as a patron seeking solace among the shelves, but as a library assistant ready to immerse myself in the world behind the circulation desk.

Mrs. Cristina Garcia, the chief librarian with a reputation for an unyielding commitment to order, greeted me with a nod. Her straight face conveyed a sense of professionalism that hinted at the standards she expected from her assistants. Today, she would guide me through the maze of responsibilities that came with the role.

We embarked on a thorough tour of the library, Mrs. Cristina pointing out the Dewey Decimal System, the reference section, and the labyrinthine stacks of fiction and non-fiction. Each section held a wealth of knowledge, and I couldn't help but feel a surge of excitement at the prospect of diving into this literary realm every day.

"Your duties are simple, Ms. Rory," Mrs. Cristina explained in a measured tone. "You'll be responsible for shelving returned books, assisting patrons in locating materials, and maintaining order within the library."

I listened attentively, absorbing the details of my responsibilities. Early shifts at seven in the morning until four in the afternoon on Mondays to Thursdays, a lunch break at 11:30, water breaks permitted in the staff room, and an unwavering commitment to silence within the library's sacred halls. The rules were straightforward, a symphony of guidelines to ensure the harmony of this literary haven.

A small sigh of relief escaped me when Mrs. Cristina handed me my ID—a golden ticket granting access to the various corners of the library. The three maroon polo shirts neatly folded beside it were my uniform, the symbol of my new role as a guardian of knowledge.

Changing into my uniform in the staff room, I looked at myself in the mirror, maroon polo neatly pressed, ID hanging from my neck. A deep breath steadied my nerves, and I felt a surge of determination. I was ready to embrace this responsibility.

The library hummed with activity as I took my place behind the circulation desk. With each shelved book and guided patron, I could feel the echoes of my brother's laughter dancing in the quiet spaces. I imagined him looking down with a proud smile, his approval, a silent encouragement as I navigated the intricacies of my newfound role.

Throughout the day, I navigated the aisles, answered inquiries, and maintained the delicate balance of quietude. In the staff room, I took my water breaks, the refreshing sips a brief respite from the pages of responsibilities.

As the day unfolded, I couldn't shake the feeling that I was creating my own narrative amidst the shelves. The library had become a canvas for new beginnings. With each hushed step, I carried the weight of responsibility and the promise of making a difference in this haven of words.

The afternoon sun cast a warm glow over the library, illuminating the rows of neatly shelved books. As I worked through the stacks, arranging volumes with a practiced rhythm, my eyes caught a familiar face in the general knowledge section. There, sitting on the floor amidst the treasure trove of information, was Walker.

Surprise flickered in both our eyes as we exchanged greetings. "Hey, Walker. What are you doing here?" I asked, a genuine smile playing on my lips.

"I just finished shelving books on that side," he pointed with a grin, his eyes gleaming with a shared sense of discovery. "And now I'm tired."

I chuckled, realizing the irony of two tired souls finding solace in the library's embrace. Walker's presence felt like a serendipitous twist in the narrative of my day, a welcome surprise that eased the weight on my shoulders.

As we shared a brief conversation amidst the shelves, I noticed the maroon polo shirt he was wearing – the same uniform as mine. It clicked. Walker also worked at the library.

"You work here too?" I asked, my surprise evident.

"Yeah! Just joined today. Figured it would be a good way to spend the summer. Plus, books are my thing," he explained, his eyes twinkling with enthusiasm.

I nodded in agreement, feeling a sense of camaraderie in our shared love for the written word. The world, it seemed, was conspiring to weave unexpected connections.

By the time the clock struck 4 PM, signaling the end of our shifts, Walker offered to walk me home. I agreed, realizing that the walk could be a chance for us to get to know each other beyond the library's confines.

As we strolled through the exit, Walker greeted Mrs. Cristina with cheerful enthusiasm. "Bye, Mrs. Cristina!"

However, Mrs. Cristina, engrossed in her work, seemed to be in a world of her own, her response lost in the silence of the library. Walker chuckled beside me. "Is she always like that?" I asked, curious about the enigmatic chief librarian.

"Nah, she's a sweetheart," Walker responded with a grin, his optimism a contagious force. "She just gets lost in the world of books sometimes."

I couldn't help but smile at his unwavering positivity. It was as if Walker, with his boundless energy, had become a beacon of light in the quiet corridors of the library.

Walker walked me home, the conversation flowing effortlessly between us. As we approached my doorstep, a sense of gratitude welled up within me. The library, once a place of solitude, had become the setting for unexpected connections and shared stories.

"Thanks for walking me home, Walker," I said, my appreciation evident in my eyes.

He grinned, his presence a reminder that sometimes, in the most unexpected corners of life, we find the companionship we didn't know we needed. As he bid me farewell, the echoes of laughter and shared secrets lingered in the air. The chapters of my day had unfolded in ways I couldn't have predicted, and for the first time in a long while, I felt a glimmer of hope amidst the pages of my life.

7

A Friend

The first week at the library unfolded like a well-crafted story, each day adding a new chapter to the narrative of my summer. Walker, with his infectious enthusiasm and love for books, became the unexpected protagonist who made the pages come alive.

Working around books was a revelation that whispered to the core of my soul. The quiet rustle of pages, the hushed footsteps, and the gentle hum of the library felt like a symphony of serenity. It was a haven where stories unfolded beyond the confines of printed words.

Lunch breaks with Walker became a cherished routine. We'd escape to the back of the library, facing a small pond that mirrored the tranquility within. The moments spent in shared silence or engaged in easy conversation made the weight on my shoulders feel a little lighter. His presence was a balm to the solitude I had grown accustomed to.

The sun spilled its golden warmth across the library courtyard as Walker and I found our familiar spot at the back. The rhythmic rustling of pages and distant murmurs of students provided a soothing background to our shared moments of respite.

"What's your dream job, Rory?" Walker inquired; his eyes genuinely curious. It was one of those simple questions that opened the door to revealing the intricacies of our aspirations.

I pondered for a moment, slicing through my sandwich with contemplative ease.

"Honestly, I don't have one specific dream job," I admitted. "There are so many things I want to do. I love working at the library, and someday, I dream of opening a cozy cafe. Maybe work with a charity organization, or pen down my thoughts as a writer."

Walker's smile widened; his eyes gleaming with admiration. "That's quite a list. You've got a lot you want to accomplish."

I chuckled, savoring the blend of flavors from my lunch. "Yeah, I guess. What about you, Walker? Any dreams or plans for the future?"

He shook his head, a soft smile playing on his lips. "I really still don't know."

I respected his honesty, sensing an air of uncertainty that lingered in his response. Instead of pressing further, I changed the subject, steering away from the depths that might make him uncomfortable.

We continued our lunchtime ritual, engrossed in a debate about whether pineapples belong on pizzas.

Thursday afternoon, as we walked home, our conversation veered into the realm of Harry Potter. It was a shared love that added another layer to our growing connection. As Walker animatedly discussed his favorite scenes, I couldn't help but marvel at the simplicity of the joy I felt in that moment.

"I was devastated when Sirius died," Walker confessed, his

eyes reflecting the genuine emotion tied to the fictional world. "He was one of my favorites."

"I know, mine too," I replied, my heart resonating with the shared pain of fictional loss. "And Draco… I felt bad for him. Forced into things he didn't want to do."

"True. So, who's your favorite villain in the series?"

"Voldemort, no doubt," I answered. "Classic, ominous, and a symbol of pure evil."

Walker nodded, contemplating the choice. "Interesting. Mine's Bellatrix Lestrange."

I raised an eyebrow, intrigued. "Really? She's quite ruthless."

He grinned, "Exactly. There's something fascinating about her."

As we approached the topic of Hogwarts houses, I couldn't help but wonder about Walker's preferences. "What house would you want to be in?"

"Gryffindor, no hesitation. The bravest and boldest," he declared with a grin.

I playfully nudged his shoulder. "Classic choice. I'd go for Slytherin."

A mock look of hurt flashed across Walker's face. "Slytherin? You don't want to be bunkmates?"

I laughed, realizing my oversight. "Oh, come on. Boys and girls don't share the same rooms at Hogwarts, you know."

Walker feigned a dramatic sigh.

As we approached my doorstep, a sudden burst of courage propelled me to extend an invitation. "Will you come with me to the lake tomorrow?" I blurted out, immediately feeling a flush of embarrassment.

Walker's smile widened, his eyes reflecting the joy of being invited. "I would love to," he said, teasing me gently. "Not that

I don't have plans on a Friday or anything."

I blushed, stammering through my words. "I mean, it's summer, and you might have other things—"

"I would love to," Walker repeated, his sincerity putting my nerves at ease.

Outside my house, we bid each other goodbyes, and as Walker disappeared down the street, I couldn't ignore the frantic drumming of my heart. The simple act of inviting him to the lake felt like a momentous step, a bridge connecting the solitude of my past with the companionship of my present.

As I entered my house, the echoes of laughter and shared stories lingered in the air. The library, the pond, the conversations—they all contributed to a summer that felt more than just a series of days. It was a chapter of my life unfolding with unexpected joy, and I couldn't wait to see where the pages would take me next.

8

Guilt

The sun-dappled lake sparkled like a canvas of diamonds, inviting us to immerse ourselves in the joy of a carefree Friday. Walker and I had ventured to our secret haven, the lake hidden deep within the forest, ready for a day filled with laughter and newfound adventures.

Among the trees, a tire swing hung like a promise of unexplored possibilities. Walker's contagious enthusiasm bubbled forth as he encouraged me to take a leap, to try something I had never done before—to jump into the lake from the tire swing.

As I clung to the tire, the cool breeze tousling my hair, doubt crept in. What if I failed? What if I crashed into the tree? Walker's encouragement cut through my hesitations.

"You can do it!" he cheered, his voice a reassuring melody. "Trust me. When I say jump, let go of the tire swing and jump!"

Closing my eyes, I nodded, gripping the rope tighter. Walker's voice became my anchor in that moment of anticipation. One, two, three. The tire swing moved, my heart raced, and then, with Walker's signal, I jumped.

The world blurred around me as I plunged into the refreshing embrace of the lake. The initial shock gave way to a surge of exhilaration, a thrill that traveled through every fiber of my being. When I surfaced, laughter bubbled out of me, mingling with the sounds of the forest.

Walker, his laughter echoing in the trees, followed suit. He swung into the water, and together we emerged, a symphony of joy playing out in the secluded alcove.

We spent the afternoon in pure, carefree bliss, our laughter echoing through the trees as we swung in the tire swing multiple times, releasing joyful screams with each swing. The world seemed to disappear in those moments, leaving only the sound of our shared laughter.

After countless turns on the tire swing, we decided to cool off in the lake. Walker, always the patient teacher, showed me how to lay on my back and float. The gentle waves cradled me as I looked up at the vast expanse of the sky. It was a serene moment, and for the first time, I truly appreciated the beauty of the world from a floating perspective.

We eventually made our way to a picnic blanket spread out on the grassy shore. A towel covered our damp bodies as we sat, sharing a bag of chips. The crunching of the chips mingled with the sounds of nature around us.

I mused about adopting a dog, contemplating names. "If I get one, I'd name it Fluffy," I said, a playful glint in my eyes.

Walker chuckled. "Fluffy, like the three-headed dog in Harry Potter? Nice choice. I'd name mine Snuffles, like Sirius Black's nickname."

We continued to share stories and dreams, our conversation weaving seamlessly between reality and the magical world of Harry Potter.

After a few snacks here and there, the day unfolded with

shared laughter and the playful exchange of splashes. We became children of the lake, embracing the freedom that danced on the water's surface. And then, in a moment that felt like an unwritten chapter, I did something unexpected.

Gathering the courage, I wrapped my arms around Walker's neck. He reciprocated, holding onto me as if we were two souls tethered by the simple act of embracing the moment. We lingered in that shared space, smiles exchanged like secrets only the lake could keep.

The sun dipped lower on the horizon, casting a golden glow over the water. In that quiet embrace, surrounded by the echoes of laughter and the rustle of leaves, I marveled at the courage I had found within myself. The lake had become a backdrop to a day that transcended ordinary boundaries, a day that felt like the beginning of something beautiful.

As we eventually pulled away, the laughter lingering in the air, Walker and I exchanged a look – a silent acknowledgment of the shared joy that had unfolded on the canvas of the lake. The tire swing, once a symbol of uncertainty, had become a doorway to a world where laughter echoed, and hearts dared to take a leap of joy.

The fading sunlight cast a warm glow on the quiet street as Walker and I bid each other goodnight. Despite the invitation for dinner, he mentioned needing to head home. We exchanged smiles, a silent understanding that the day at the lake had been something special.

As I stepped into the empty house, the laughter from earlier echoed in my mind. The walls seemed to retain the traces of joy, yet an emptiness lingered within me. I changed into more comfortable clothes, the smile on my face belying the turmoil beneath the surface.

A sudden surge of courage led me to Harper's room. Opening the door felt like stepping into a realm frozen in time. The room, unchanged since his departure, held the whispers of memories. I sat on the edge of his bed, fingers grazing the familiar covers.

"Hey, Harper," I whispered, the words carried away by the silence. "I miss you."

And then, as if the weight of the day gave way to a floodgate of emotions, my composure crumbled. Tears streamed down my face, an unspoken confession to the brother whose absence still cast shadows over my existence.

The dichotomy of my emotions overwhelmed me. How could I laugh and smile when the specter of guilt loomed so heavily? I was out, having fun with a guy I barely knew, while Harper's room remained untouched, a shrine to the void he left behind.

Guilt and shame gripped my heart, tearing through the veneer of happiness that had briefly adorned my day. Was I allowed to feel joy after everything I had done? The laughter at the lake seemed to mock the weight of my sins.

As I sank into Harper's bed, the realization hit me with a crushing force. The week of feeling better, the moments shared with Walker, they couldn't erase the reality of my actions. I was the reason Harper got into that car accident, the reason his room remained a frozen snapshot of the past.

"I'm sorry, I'm so sorry," I whispered, my voice choking with sobs. The words were an inadequate offering to the void, a plea for forgiveness that hung unanswered in the air.

The room, once a sanctuary, now felt like a chamber of penance. The walls, adorned with memories, seemed to close in on me. The weight of guilt bore down, a relentless reminder that happiness was a fleeting illusion in the face of irreversible mistakes.

In the silence of Harper's room, I surrendered to the torrents of remorse, the echoes of laughter replaced by the haunting whispers of regret. The journey toward healing, it seemed, demanded not just the acknowledgment of pain but also the confrontation of the shadows that lingered within.

9

Relapse

The weekend unfolded in a cocoon of solitude, and I found myself retreating to the familiar refuge of Harper's room. His bed cradled the weight of my emotions, offering a semblance of comfort. I didn't know if it was possible, but the room seemed to carry the lingering scent of him—a scent that both soothed and tormented.

Half-past five on Sunday marked a gentle pull to reality. A pang of hunger nudged me from the comfort of Harper's bed. Cereals in the cupboard beckoned, but a quick inventory revealed a shortage of milk. The convenience store, just a few steps away, promised a solution.

I grabbed my purse, a simple act that carried an unspoken acknowledgment of the void left by Harper's absence. The stares from passersby as I stepped outside were a silent commentary, a collective sympathy woven into the fabric of their glances.

The convenience store, usually a mundane refectory, became a stage for whispers and exchanged glances. I felt the weight of their judgment, the unspoken condolences that hung heavy in the air.

"Such a tragic thing for a great young man."

"I heard it was his sister."

"Poor Harper. Who would've thought."

"It's been a year, is it?"

The murmurs trailed me as I navigated the aisles, a silent chorus that underscored the tragedy of a life cut short. I grabbed two boxes of milk, avoiding eye contact with the strangers who held opinions veiled in pity.

At the counter, I felt the weight of their gaze, the unspoken questions lingering between the beeps of the cash register. I paid quickly, the jingling of coins a fleeting reminder of the world beyond Harper's room.

The walk home, a short distance filled with unspoken judgments, felt longer than usual. Each step echoed the heaviness within me. As I closed the door behind me, the silence of the house enveloped me once more. The milk, a small victory in the face of unwarranted sympathy, felt like a token of normalcy in a world now defined by tragedy.

Returning to Harper's room, boxes of milk in hand, I realized that even the simplest tasks now carried the weight of judgment. The room, with its familiar scent and the memories etched into the walls, became both a sanctuary and a reminder—a place where I sought solace, yet confronted the echoes of a world forever altered.

In the quiet solitude that followed, I poured the milk over the cereal in a ritualistic act that felt both mundane and poignant. The whispers of the world outside lingered, but within the walls of Harper's room, I found a brief respite from the judgments that clung to my every step.

Monday morning unfolded with the weight of tardiness. I hurried through the library's entrance, my footsteps echoing a hasty rhythm that clashed with the measured quietude. Mrs. Cristina, the guardian of order, met me with disappointment etched across her face. Five minutes late, and her disapproval hung heavy in the air. I mumbled a quick apology, my words a whisper carried away by the stern gaze of the chief librarian.

In the staff room, I left my belongings, an unspoken acknowledgment of the misstep. The day unfolded in an uneventful rhythm; my efforts focused on the tasks at hand. I avoided seeking out Walker, the embodiment of everything good in a world now tainted by guilt. He, like Harper, was a beacon of sunshine, an epitome of goodness that I feared tainting with my presence.

As I maneuvered through the journals and magazines, my peripheral vision caught Walker's friendly greeting. "Hey!" he called out, his voice a ray of warmth cutting through the hushed ambiance. However, I opted for a swift U-turn, dropping my gaze and walking away as if I hadn't heard or seen him. The distance I imposed felt like a protective barrier, shielding him from the shadows that clung to my existence.

The afternoon brought with it a sense of anticipation as I approached the library's exit. Walker, seemingly waiting for me, stood just outside. But instead of acknowledging his presence, I quickened my pace, leaving him behind. Each step carried the weight of avoidance, the echoes of guilt that drove me away from the flicker of goodness I saw in him.

The world beyond the library felt quieter, the solitude offering a refuge from the complications that threatened to unravel within. As I walked home, the shadows of avoidance clung to me, a silent testament to the internal turmoil that had taken root. The echoes of "hey" lingered in the air, unanswered and unheard, a symbol of the barriers I had erected to protect the goodness I believed I didn't deserve.

10

This is me trying

The lake, once sanctuary, now seemed to mirror the complexities of my emotions. Friday morning arrived with quiet solitude, the sun casting a gentle glow upon the water. I sat alone by the shore, the ripples of the lake mirroring the turmoil within.

The week had been a relentless battle with myself, the pain of avoiding Walker, a constant companion. In my misguided belief that distancing myself would spare him from the darkness I carried, I pushed him away. Maybe, I thought, he would realize that I wasn't worth the effort, that my company was a burden he didn't need. It would be for the best, a self-imposed isolation to protect him from the shadows that clung to my soul.

Lost in contemplation, the crunch of twigs at a distance jolted me from my thoughts. I turned my head to see Walker approaching, his presence a disruption to the solitude I sought. Panic seized me, and I stood quickly, attempting to walk away. But Walker, kind and compassionate as ever, held his hands up, a silent plea not to force me into anything.

"I don't know what happened, I don't know why you're

avoiding me," he said, his voice a soothing melody that cut through the tension. "But I want you to know, whatever it is you're going through, I'm here."

Tears welled up in my eyes, the compassion in his words breaking through the walls I had constructed around myself. Walker's next words echoed like a promise in the quiet morning air. "You can ignore me, Rory, but I'm not going away."

His unwavering support, the kindness in his eyes, almost tempted me to abandon the walls I had built. I stood there, on the precipice of reaching out for comfort and warmth, but fear held me in place. I couldn't look at him, or I would break. The vulnerability threatening to surface, I chose to leave without looking back.

The sound of my retreating footsteps echoed in the stillness of the morning. Walker's words lingered in the air, a promise that hung like a delicate thread between us. The lake, witness to the internal struggles that unfolded on its shores, held the echoes of avoidance and the untold emotions that lingered beneath the surface.

The library held a peculiar atmosphere in the following week, one tinted with the shadows of avoidance and the yearning for connection. Walker remained a constant presence, offering small smiles from a distance but never pushing himself into my guarded world. His considerate gestures were a silent acknowledgment of the space I needed, a space I had created to protect him from the shadows that clung to my existence.

Sometimes, in the quiet aisles, I would feel Walker walk past me, our shoulders brushing in a subtle dance of proximity. Each touch sent a ripple through my heart, a yearning to bridge the distance and delve into the warmth he emanated. The desire to talk to him, to be near him, tugged at the edges of my consciousness like an unresolved melody.

Yet, the shadows of guilt and doubt cast their pall over the possibility of connection. Would Walker still accept me if he knew the truth? Would the stains on my past taint the purity of his soul? The questions lingered, a silent debate within myself.

As I shelved books and tended to the duties in the library, my eyes occasionally met Walker's across the room. The unspoken understanding in his gaze hinted at a willingness to wait, a patience that both comforted and pained me. His kindness, a beacon of light in the dimness of my world, begged the question of whether I deserved it.

The internal struggle continued, a battle between the desire for connection and the fear of tarnishing something pure. I missed Walker, missed the laughter and warmth he brought into my life. Yet, the hesitation to expose the shadows within held me back.

The library, with its silent shelves and quiet corners, became a theater of contemplation. The echoes of footsteps and hushed whispers seemed to underscore the unspoken dialogue between Walker and me. Each passing day brought the temptation to reach out and the fear of pushing him away.

In the dance of shadows and yearning, the library became a space where the weight of the past and the longing for connection collided. Walker, a beacon of kindness, remained a distant yet persistent presence, leaving me to grapple with the question of whether the shadows within could coexist with the light he offered.

Thursday afternoon, the library held a peculiar weight, the weight of unspoken words lingering between the shelves. As the day waned, the decision to approach Walker took root within me like a quiet storm. The invitation to breakfast by the lake hung in the air, a tentative gesture toward connection.

I found Walker among the shelves, his eyes lighting up at the prospect of an invitation.

"Hi," I whispered. "Uhm, I was wondering if you would like to have breakfast with me by the lake tomorrow."

He composed himself, a subtle attempt to mask the joy that flickered in his gaze. "Breakfast by the lake sounds wonderful," he replied, a restrained enthusiasm tingling his voice.

The words left a bittersweet taste in my mouth. The excitement in Walker's eyes mirrored the warmth he brought into my life. But beneath the surface, a conflict brewed. It was unfair for him to remain in the dark, to believe that I was as good as he was. The shadows that clung to my past needed acknowledgment, and Walker deserved to know the truth.

As I stood there, contemplating the invitation that hung in the air, a resolve solidified within me. I couldn't keep him in the dark any longer. It was time to come clean, to reveal the shadows that lurked within the recesses of my life. If Walker chose to walk away, it would be for the best, a self-imposed salvation for him. He deserved to be free from the weight of my secrets.

The walk to the lake the next morning would be more than just a casual breakfast. It would be an unveiling, a chance for Walker to see past the facade I had carefully constructed. The internal debate raged on, torn between the desire for honesty and the fear of rejection.

Yet, somewhere deep in my bones, a yearning persisted. I wanted Walker to stay, to see beyond the shadows and still want to be a part of my life. The conflicting desires swirled within me as the decision to invite him became a commitment to confronting the truths I had hidden.

As Thursday faded into Friday, the weight of anticipation settled in my chest. The shadows cast by my past and the longing for connection collided, creating a tumultuous landscape within me. The lake, once a place of solace, now stood as a threshold where the shadows within me would be unveiled, and the fate of the connection between Walker and me would be decided.

11

My Past

The morning air whispered through the trees as I approached the lake, the dappled sunlight creating a serene atmosphere. Walker was already there, a solitary figure by the water, unaware of my presence. I lingered at a distance, watching him with a sense of both admiration and trepidation.

He was handsome, not just in appearance but in the way his kindness radiated from within. Walker's soul seemed to shine brighter than the morning sun, and I couldn't help but marvel at the purity he brought into my life. The desire to keep him, to have him see past the shadows that clung to me, pulsed within me like an erratic heartbeat.

Walker, lost in the tranquility of the lake, looked around, and our eyes met. A flush painted his cheeks as he stood, the realization of my presence sinking in. With a warm smile, he greeted me, and I felt a mixture of nervousness and gratitude.

I raised the small picnic basket in my hands, a humble offering for the morning rendezvous. Inside were ham and cheese sandwiches, carefully prepared for both of us, and a jug of orange juice to complement the simple feast.

"Good morning," Walker said, his eyes reflecting a genuine joy that sent a gentle warmth through me. As I closed the distance between us, the echoes of the lake seemed to underscore the vulnerability of the moment.

"Good morning," I replied, a tentative smile playing on my lips. The unspoken weight of the shadows lingered beneath the surface, but for now, the lake held the promise of a shared morning, a chance to bridge the gaps between us.

The sun continued its ascent, casting a golden glow over the water. As we settled by the shore, the small picnic basket between us, the gentle lapping of the lake seemed to echo the rhythm of a conversation waiting to unfold. The ham and cheese sandwiches became a metaphor for the simplicity I yearned for, a connection untainted by the shadows that lingered in the corners of my past.

In that moment, with the water gently embracing the shore, I chose to savor the fragile beauty of the morning. The complexities of the shadows would come to light in due time, but for now, there was the warmth of the sun, the gentle ripple of the lake, and the shared silence that held the promise of connection.

The gentle lapping of the lake seemed to hold its breath as Walker and I sat in the quietude, sharing the modest breakfast I had prepared. The ham and cheese sandwiches became a subtle bridge between us, a small offering in the hushed morning light.

Silence enveloped us, and I could sense Walker's understanding. He didn't press me to speak, a compassionate acknowledgment of the delicate nature of the moment. The unspoken warmth between us was a silent reassurance that he was here, patiently waiting for the shadows I was about to reveal.

I took a deep breath, my gaze fixed on the rippling water. "I need to tell you something," I began, my voice a fragile echo in the stillness. "And I'll understand if you decide to walk away after hearing it."

Walker nodded, his full attention on me.

"Over a year ago, I started dating a guy named Tom at school. I was drawn to the attention and flattery he offered. Tom made me feel that I was seen, even if the attention came with an undercurrent of discomfort." I paused, glancing at Walker whose attentive demeanor didn't wane. "But Harper, my protective older brother, saw through the facade. He disapproved of Tom, sensing the prick beneath the charm. For the first time, anger flared between us. I never questioned Harper's dating history, but when he voiced concern, I lashed out in frustration."

I closed my eyes and took a deep breath. I was never able to relay this story before out loud.

"One night," I continued, "Tom's true intentions emerged cruelly. During a party, he revealed that our entire relationship was a bet, a game to win a wager. The revelation left me shattered, and I couldn't contain the pain and anger. I slapped Tom, a desperate attempt to reclaim an impression of control. That night, rain poured heavily, mirroring the storm within me. Feeling low and broken, I called Harper to pick me up, a cry for help in the darkest hour. Past midnight, in the midst of the downpour, Harper rushed to my aid. He loved me unconditionally, and I stood there in the rain, crying, waiting for the brother who never came."

Walker took my hand in his as if he knew where the story was going. I took this as my motivation to continue, to let this all out—a burden in my heart that I was never able to share.

"The harsh reality unfolded with a devastating twist. Harper, on his way to rescue me, got into a car accident. The tragedy was the consequence of his selfless act, an attempt to shield his little sister from the mistakes she made."

Tears welled in my eyes as the weight of the past hung heavily in the air. I couldn't look at Walker. The echoes of that rain-soaked night, the pain, the regret—they reverberated in the silent morning, a poignant testament to the price paid for misguided choices.

I looked up, meeting Walker's eyes. In their depths, I found only kindness and compassion. He wasn't going anywhere. The warmth of his hand, the steadiness of his gaze, became an anchor in the tempest of emotions swirling within me.

A sob escaped me, the tears that had been held back for far too long now streaming down my cheeks. Walker's presence, his simple gesture of holding my hand, allowed me to release the pent-up emotions that had been haunting the corridors of my heart.

With a shaky breath, I continued my story. It was my father who picked me up that night after Tom's betrayal. Together, we rushed to the hospital, where the harsh reality awaited. My mother clung to Harper's hands, covered in blood, her wails filling the sterile air. The image was etched in my memory—a devastating tableau of loss and grief.

That was the moment I knew Harper was gone. A memory I tried to push away, for the pain it carried was too overwhelming. The guilt gnawed at me—if Harper had stayed home instead of rushing to pick me up, he might still be alive today. He could have been here, in this very lake, and I could introduce Walker to him. They would get along, I was sure of it, for they were both beautiful souls.

The weight of the revelation hung heavy between us, the lake mirroring the depth of the emotions stirred by the narrative. Yet, Walker remained by my side, a steady presence in the tempest of regret and sorrow.

As the morning unfolded, the echoes of the past merged with the ripples on the lake. Walker's hand remained entwined with mine, a silent promise of support and understanding. In that shared moment of vulnerability, I realized that some wounds may never fully heal, but the gentle compassion of another soul could offer solace in the journey of acceptance and healing.

Time hung suspended in the hushed morning air as I allowed the weight of my past to spill forth, tears flowing freely in the presence of Walker's unwavering support. He remained by my side, a steady anchor in the storm of emotions that had long been suppressed.

I took my time, each sob an echo of the pain I had carried within. Walker, a compassionate witness to my vulnerability, never once left my side. When the tears finally subsided, he gently took my face in his hands, his touch tender and comforting. His thumb brushed away the remnants of sorrow etched on my cheeks.

"I'm not sure if anyone has told you this, but it's not your fault," Walker spoke softly, his words weaving through the fragile quiet between us. "Your brother chose to go to you because he loved you. The accident was terrible. It was tragic. No one wanted that, and it's not your fault."

A protest lingered on my lips, but Walker silenced it with a gentle kiss on my forehead. The warmth of his lips left an imprint, a healing balm on the wounds that time had failed to mend. His reassurance echoed like a soothing melody, a promise of understanding and acceptance.

"If your brother were here," Walker continued, his voice a whisper that resonated in the stillness, "he would tell you the same."

My heart swelled with gratitude for Walker, for his unwavering presence and the gentle words that sought to mend the fractures within.

Someday, I hoped to believe Walker's words—to accept that Harper's choice to come to my aid was an expression of love, not a burden of blame. The journey toward healing lay ahead, and Walker, with his compassionate embrace, had become an unexpected guide along the path of acceptance and self-forgiveness.

As we sat by the lake, the echoes of my brother's memory and the gentle whispers of Walker's reassurance intertwined. The healing had only just begun, but in the quiet morning, I found a flicker of hope that someday, I might embrace the truth in Walker's words and find peace within the echoes of the past.

12

Happiness

In the days that followed the unveiling of my past, a subtle transformation began to ripple through the fabric of my existence. The weight that had tethered me to the shadows seemed to lift, and each interaction with Walker became a brushstroke of warmth on the canvas of my healing heart.

Walker and I found solace in the shared spaces of the library, where our conversations flowed freely like the pages of the books that surrounded us. Lunch breaks became a cherished ritual, an opportunity to share stories and laughter that resonated with newfound lightness.

There was a noticeable shift in Walker's demeanor. His affectionate gestures became more pronounced, a silent declaration of his steadfast presence. As we strolled through the streets, he would take my hand, fingers intertwining in a gentle dance that echoed the growing connection between us.

On one of our lunch breaks, Walker and I sat at our usual spot at the back of the library. Unbeknownst to me, Walker had a little surprise in store.

He handed me a cup of mint chocolate ice cream, and my eyes

widened in delight. "How did you know?" I squealed, unable to hide my excitement.

"What do you mean?" Walker asked, a hint of innocence in his eyes.

"That I love mint chocolate?" I replied, my smile widening.

Walker grinned, "Mint chocolate is a special flavor, just like you. I thought it suited you because you're one of a kind."

I blushed, feeling the warmth spread across my cheeks. Walker always had a way of surprising me, and this thoughtful gesture was no exception. Teasingly, I remarked, "I didn't know you were so corny."

Walker chuckled, "Well, consider it a unique flavor for a unique person." As we enjoyed our ice cream, the library seemed to fade away, leaving only the sweetness of the moment between us.

That afternoon, as I immersed myself in the meticulous task of checking a list of borrowed books, Walker breezed past me. In a sudden, unexpected moment, he took my hand and planted a soft kiss on it. I was momentarily taken aback, my cheeks flushing with surprise. When I looked up, Walker met my gaze with a mischievous wink, a playful acknowledgment of the newfound lightness that danced between us.

A genuine smile tugged at the corners of my lips. Walker's gestures, his warmth, and the playful spontaneity of that kiss became a beacon of joy in the landscape of my healing heart. The weight of guilt and sorrow seemed to dissipate in the presence of his kindness, and for the first time in a long while, I began to feel good about the prospect of embracing joy.

The library, once a sanctuary of solitude, transformed into a space where shared laughter echoed. Each step taken with Walker felt like a stride toward a brighter horizon. In the subtle nuances of affection and the genuine connection we cultivated, I found the promise of healing and the gentle whispers of a heart learning to beat in harmony with the symphony of life.

13

A Promise

As the weeks unfolded in the gentle embrace of newfound companionship, I couldn't help but reflect on the transformation that had taken root in my life. The library had become a haven of shared laughter, and the days felt lighter, like the sun breaking through after a storm. Perhaps, in the subtle threads of time, God had been weaving the fulfillment of my birthday wish—for everything to be okay.

The weight that had burdened my heart seemed to dissipate, replaced by the warmth of Walker's companionship and the joy we found in each other's presence. It wasn't an instant fix, but the gradual mending of my spirit mirrored the dawning light of a new day.

One Friday morning, as sunlight filtered through the curtains, I heard a series of excited knocks on my door. When I opened it, there stood Walker, a backpack slung over his shoulder and what appeared to be a tent bag in his hand.

"Surprise!" he exclaimed, his eyes sparkling with infectious enthusiasm. "Now go get changed, and we're going on an adventure."

A smile spread across my face, reaching ear to ear. Walker had a way of surprising me every single day, and each unexpected gesture added another layer of color to my life.

"What adventure?" I asked, curiosity bubbling in my voice.

"We're going camping!" Walker declared; his excitement contagious.

At that moment, as Walker stood at my doorstep, I realized that I was no longer alone, no longer lonely. His presence had become a constant, a source of light and joy that dispelled the shadows that had lingered for far too long.

As I changed into more suitable attire for our camping adventure, I marveled at the newfound warmth that had nestled into my heart. Walker's surprises had become a beacon of joy, and the prospect of a camping trip further solidified the bond we were weaving together.

The journey toward healing continued, but with each step, I felt a deep sense of gratitude for the unexpected gifts that had manifested in my life. Walker, with his kind heart and the adventure he brought to my doorstep, had become a reminder that even in the aftermath of tragedy, there could be moments of joy and companionship that stitched together the broken pieces into resilience and hope.

The morning unfolded like a delicate flower, and I found myself perched on a makeshift seat, watching with admiration as Walker expertly set up the pretty blue tent. Its hue reminded me of the one that had adorned Harper's room, the same one that had sheltered us during weekends by the lake. Harper used to be the one skillfully arranging the tent, and I, like a princess, would sit and marvel at his handiwork.

Now, here was Walker, his hands moving with practiced ease, a huge smile illuminating his face. "You're so good at this," I marveled, my appreciation evident in the lilt of my voice.

Walker chuckled, a twinkle in his eyes. "Well, this is just one of my many talents."

My laughter bubbled forth, filling the space between us with a melody of joy. The familiarity of the moment, the echoes of shared memories, cast a spell of warmth around us. However, beneath the surface, a realization blossomed. Amidst all the conversations we'd shared, we'd never delved into Walker's past, his family, or the intricacies that made him who he was.

A pang of guilt whispered through me—had our interactions become a one-sided exchange, revolving solely around my troubles? Determination sparked within me a newfound mission to bridge the gap and unveil the layers of the person who had brought so much light into my life.

"Where did you learn all this?" I asked, my voice carrying a hint of curiosity. I wanted Walker to know that I was interested in him, in the stories that shaped his world.

Walker's expression shifted momentarily, a subtle shadow crossing his face before disappearing as swiftly as it had arrived. "In my old school," he replied with a smile. "I was in the Boy Scouts."

The revelation hung in the air, and I sensed there was more beneath the surface. Still, I respected the unspoken boundaries and chose not to pry further. Instead, I let the information settle, appreciating the glimpse into Walker's past.

As the tent stood proudly, a symbol of shared endeavors and the promise of a camping adventure, I realized that in the delicate dance of getting to know one another, every revelation, no matter how small, was a step toward deeper understanding. Walker had opened a door to his past, and as we embarked on our camping escapade, I couldn't help but anticipate the tales and adventures that would unfold, both under the canvas sky and in the shared moments between us.

The lake embraced us with its refreshing coolness as Walker and I reveled in the simple joys of plunging into the water from the tire swing. Laughter echoed through the air; a harmonious melody that resonated with the spirits of carefree days gone by. As the sun began its descent, casting a warm glow upon the horizon, Walker took charge of starting a crackling bonfire.

With a sense of excitement, Walker opened his bag, revealing an array of delectable treats. "Just to set your expectations," he began with a playful grin, "I'm not a seasoned chef."

I giggled and opened the containers, my eyes widening in surprise at the sight of apple doughnuts, egg tarts, summer sausage rolls, and classic cheese scones. "You just bought all these!" I exclaimed.

Walker huffed in mock offense, a mischievous glint in his eyes. "Well, the summer sausage rolls are mine."

We nestled together, sharing a blanket as we indulged in the delightful feast. The evening air hummed with the crackling of the fire, the lapping of waves against the shore, and the laughter that painted the canvas of our shared experience. Marshmallows met their fate over the open flame, transforming into gooey delights that we savored under the canvas of the starlit sky.

The crackling of the campfire and the soft rustling of leaves surrounded us as Walker and I lay side by side, gazing up at the vast canvas of stars. The night sky was a blanket, a celestial masterpiece that sparked our curiosity.

I turned my head to Walker, breaking the tranquil silence. "What do you think of the stars?" I asked, my voice a mere whisper against the night.

Walker's eyes followed the constellation patterns above us. "Stars are like the people who love us but have departed this earth. They're up above, watching over us. That's why you can't count them all."

I looked at him, a playful smile dancing on my lips. I didn't entirely believe his explanation, but I loved the poetic charm in his words. Stars, people we love. "I like that," I said, my gaze returning to the sparkling night sky.

"What about you?" Walker asked, turning his attention back to me.

I pondered for a moment before answering, "Stars are celestial gifts, sprinkled across the darkness so we don't have to experience the night in total blackness. No matter how brave we are, there's something about the dark that makes us feel alone and sad. Stars are there to remind us that even in the darkest moments, there's always a glimmer of light."

Glancing at Walker, I saw a smile form in the corner of his lips.

As we continued to lay side by side, sharing our perspectives on the stars, the night seemed to wrap around us like a comforting blanket, and the glow of celestial wonders filled our hearts with a quiet warmth.

As we gazed at the stars, hand in hand, a quiet moment settled over us.

"Walker?" I spoke, breaking the peaceful silence.

"Hmm?" he replied, turning his gaze toward me.

"Thank you," I said sincerely, my words carrying the weight of gratitude.

Walker met my gaze, and in that exchange, I caught a glimpse of something deeper in his eyes—a mixture of warmth and a trace of hidden sorrow. His response to my gratitude was a gentle smile, though a hint of vulnerability lingered beneath the surface.

"Thank you," I repeated, sensing a connection between us that surpassed the spoken word. A tear escaped from Walker's left eye, silently trailing down his cheek. Without hesitation, I knew what I needed to do.

I leaned in, and to my surprise, Walker was already leaning in towards me. Our lips met in a tender kiss, a fusion of shared appreciation and a burgeoning connection. His hand found my waist, pulling me closer, while mine traveled through his hair. When we parted, a breathless space lingering between us, Walker spoke words that reverberated with promise.

"I'm not going anywhere," he declared, and I believed him. In that sacred moment beneath the stars, we found solace in each other's presence, and a bond that went beyond the scars of our individual pasts began to weave its way into our shared future.

14

Rock-bottom

Saturday morning held remnants of a joyous night spent under the stars with Walker, but as I stepped into the familiar embrace of home, the sight that greeted me shattered the fragile peace I had found.

My parents awaited me in the living room, travel bags standing sentinel by their sides. A fragile smile clung to my face; a residue of the happiness Walker had woven into my life. However, that fleeting joy crumbled when I saw the solemn expressions etched on my parents' faces.

"Rory," my father's voice carried a soft note, an attempt to quell the storm that lurked within our home. But my mother's words thundered through the air, a tempest of accusation and grief.

"Where have you been? You've been out again, haven't you? On a date? It's been a year, and you still haven't learned from your mistakes!"

"Tillie," my father interjected, attempting to temper the ferocity of my mother's words.

Tears welled up in my eyes as the weight of their disapproval settled upon me. I understood the undercurrents of my mother's anger—I had ventured out into the night, reminiscent of the ill-fated evening Harper had left our lives.

"No, Simon," my mother's tone held a venomous anger. "She is being irrational and irresponsible. She's sixteen for, Pete's sake!"

"Seventeen!" My voice sliced through the tension, my tears streaming freely. "I am seventeen."

"That doesn't make things better," my mother hissed, the edges of her anger sharpening.

"It doesn't. Nothing that's happening is making anything better. I celebrated my birthday a month ago, and you didn't even call me."

My mother's temper escalated. "Why would you think that I would want to call you? After what you did to my son?"

"He was my brother too!"

"HE IS NOT!" My mother's anger erupted, her screams echoing through the house. "HE IS NOT YOURS TO CLAIM. HE IS MY ONLY CHILD, MY BABY, AND YOU TOOK HIM FROM ME!"

"Only?" I heard the break in my voice.

Confusion clouded my mind. I struggled to comprehend the depths of my mother's fury; the unraveling of emotions that had been concealed beneath the surface. As her words reverberated through the room, I grappled with the realization that the wounds of loss had not yet begun to heal within the walls of our fractured home.

The air hung heavy with unspoken truths as I stood in the wake of my mother's revelation. "You are not my daughter. You never were." The words echoed in the hollow chambers of my mind, a stark contrast to the love and belonging I had once believed to be true.

"What do you mean?" My voice wavered into a whisper, a desperate plea for clarity in the face of a revelation that threatened to unravel the very fabric of my identity.

"TILLIE." My father's stern voice sliced through the tension, a feeble attempt to halt the torrent of revelations cascading from my mother's lips.

"You are not my daughter. You never were." My mother's words hung in the air, an accusation that cut through the remnants of the familial bond we had clung to.

"And I accepted you into my home, clothed you, gave you food. We sent you to the best school in this town. I gave you Harper, and you were everything to him. But what did you do? You ungrateful girl! YOU TOOK MY SON FROM ME. And if you think I'd rather call you on your birthdays than spend my years mourning the loss of my son, YOU ARE WRONG."

With those words, my mother seized her luggage and stormed out of the house, leaving me in the suffocating silence of an unraveling reality. My father, caught in the crossfire, stood uncertain, his gaze laden with a sorrow that mirrored my own.

"Please forgive your mom," he implored, his voice laced with a sense of helplessness. "Just don't take her words to heart. Please, honey." He kissed me on the head, a gesture that once held warmth but now carried the weight of shattered bonds, and followed my mother out of the door. "I'll call you!"

I was once again left in the cavernous emptiness of a home that had ceased to be mine. The truth, however painful, lingered in the air, unraveling the threads that had bound us together. The echoes of my mother's accusations reverberated, leaving me to grapple with the shards of a shattered identity and the profound absence of the familial love I had longed for.

The weight of my mother's words, like a torrent of heavy rain, had soaked through the fabric of my being, leaving me drenched in sorrow. Alone in the dimly lit living room, I succumbed to the overwhelming grief that had surged within me. The tears flowed freely, a silent river of despair that mirrored the storm brewing outside.

Unable to endure the haunting echoes of my mother's accusations, I crumbled onto the couch, a sanctuary that had once been a haven. Lost and misplaced in a world that seemed to have unraveled, I wept until the clock on the wall declared it to be half past midnight.

As the oppressive silence threatened to consume me, a sudden knock on the door shattered the stillness. Startled, I opened the door to find the one person I longed to see the most—Walker.

His eyes, filled with questions, softened as he took in the disarray of my tear-streaked face. Without a word, he enveloped me in a warm embrace, a sanctuary within the storm of my emotions. We sat down on the couch, his presence a comforting anchor in the tempest that raged within me.

As I poured out the fragments of my shattered world, Walker listened with a solemn understanding. The pain etched on his face mirrored the depth of my sorrow.

"I'm sorry," I whispered, the weight of guilt settling upon me like an unwelcome guest.

Walker shook his head, his hazel eyes reflecting compassion. "There's nothing to be sorry for."

But the guilt lingered, a persistent shadow that clung to my soul. What had I done to deserve someone like Walker? He held me tight, a reassuring presence that transcended words, calming the tempest within my heart. In that moment, Walker became my anchor, an angel sent to me in my darkest hour, a source of solace when the world seemed to crumble around me.

15

A Discovery

The sun painted the room in soft hues as I stirred from a restless slumber. The realization hit me like a cold wave—Walker must have left. I couldn't blame him; it was late, and the worry etched on his parents' faces lingered in my mind. I lay there for a moment, the emptiness echoing the ache within my chest.

Seeking solace, I retreated to Harper's room on that Sunday, cocooned in the familiar embrace of his bed. The weight of the past pressed upon me, and I found refuge in the memories that clung to the room like echoes of a happier time.

Monday dawned, bringing with it a hollow ache. As I resumed my duties at the library, there was an absence that loomed larger than ever—no sign of Walker. Lunch came and went, the library's quietude punctuating the unease that settled in my bones. By the late afternoon, anxiety gnawed at me. Where was he? Was he sick?

Mrs. Cristina called me over, handing me a list of newspapers stored in the archives. The task seemed mundane, a welcomed distraction from the worry that lingered. The list led me to the dusty stacks, and my fingers trembled as I reached for a newspaper from a year ago—the day after Harper's accident.

As I scanned the front page, Harper's image stared back at me, frozen in time. A tear traced a silent path down my cheek as I delicately caressed the paper, reliving the pain of that fateful day. But beneath Harper's photograph, another photo and name emerged from the shadows—Walker Louis.

* * *

Tragic Intersection Collision Claims One Life, Leaves Another in Critical Condition

In a devastating turn of events at the intersection of Maple Street and Oak Avenue last night, a violent car crash unfolded, resulting in the loss of one young life and leaving another in critical condition. Harper Grant, a 19-year-old resident of our close-knit community, and Walker Louis, 17, were involved in the collision that occurred at approximately 12:45 AM. Both individuals were immediately rushed to Mercy General Hospital for urgent medical attention. Harper Grant, known for his friendly demeanor and vibrant personality, succumbed to his injuries and was declared dead on arrival at the hospital. The 19-year-old's untimely demise has left the community in shock and mourning, as he was a well-loved member of the community, known for his infectious enthusiasm and zest for life.

Walker Louis, 17, is currently fighting for his life in the intensive care unit. The hospital staff is working tirelessly to stabilize his condition, and his family and friends anxiously await updates on his progress. Walker, a familiar face in the community, is described by those who know him as a kind-hearted and caring individual.

61

The cause of the collision remains under investigation by local authorities. Preliminary reports suggest that the incident occurred due to a disregard for traffic signals, leading to a high-impact collision that involved multiple vehicles. Eyewitnesses recount a scene of chaos as emergency services rushed to the intersection to provide immediate assistance.

The community has come together to offer support to the grieving families and send heartfelt wishes for Walker Louis's recovery.

Vigils and memorials are being organized in memory of Harper Grant, whose presence will be deeply missed by friends, family, and the community at large.

As the investigation continues, the community remains united in support, grappling with the profound loss of one young life and holding onto hope for the recovery of another.

16

Walker Louis

My hands trembled as I clutched the newspaper, the words blurring before my tear-filled eyes. Walker Louis. The name echoed in my mind, a haunting refrain that left me reeling. How could this be? Walker, the one who had brought light into my darkened world, the one who stood by me when everything crumbled, was now entangled in the shadows of tragedy.

I fumbled through the pages of subsequent newspapers, desperately seeking more information. Each turn seemed to bring a new layer of agony. The realization hit me like a sledgehammer when I found the article a week after the accident. Walker Louis, 17, succumbed to the injuries inflicted by a devastating car crash, a week-long battle against the grasp of death that ultimately claimed him.

"No, no," I gasped, the world around me spiraling into chaos I couldn't comprehend. It was too much, too painful to accept. Walker, my beacon of solace, was now a part of the tragic narrative that had taken my brother away.

I read through the article through a haze of tears, absorbing the harsh reality. Walker Louis had been intoxicated on the night of the accident, careening through the streets at a reckless speed that collided with Harper's life. The same hands that had held mine in comfort, the same eyes that had glistened with kindness, were now stained with the consequences of a devastating choice.

Guilt, confusion, and grief intertwined, creating an indescribable torment within me. How could I not have known? How could Walker keep this from me? I felt the weight of my own ignorance and the darkness that Walker had concealed behind his warm smile and comforting presence.

The room seemed to close in on me as I clutched the newspaper, the truth too heavy to bear. The Walker I thought I knew was entangled in a web of shadows, and the lines between right and wrong, solace and despair, blurred into a chaotic tangle of emotions.

My footsteps echoed in my ears as I hurriedly left the library, the world around me a chaotic blur. Tears streamed down my face, a manifestation of the turmoil within my shattered soul. The weight of betrayal, confusion, and grief bore down on me as I made my way to the lake—a place that had once been a sanctuary of solace, now transformed into the stage for my unraveling reality.

The journey to the lake felt like an eternity, my mind a whirlwind of shattered thoughts. The universe seemed to mock me, as if every step was a reminder of the pain that had been concealed beneath the surface of my newfound happiness.

When the lake finally came into view, Walker stood there with his hands in his pockets, his back turned to me. My breath caught in my throat, and I approached him cautiously, my heart pounding against the walls of my chest. Questions, accusations, and hurt burned in my eyes as I confronted the one who had become my confidant, my friend, my solace.

His slow turn brought him to face me, and my heart plummeted. Walker's eyes, bloodshot red and teary, met mine. A fragile smile tugged at his lips, a feeble acknowledgment of the shattered reality we found ourselves in.

"You found it all out," he whispered, his voice carrying the weight of a truth I had yet to fully grasp. A single tear traced a path down his cheek, mirroring the torrent of emotions that had engulfed us both.

My world crumbled as the words lingered in the air, leaving us suspended in the shattered echoes of our intertwined fates.

17

The Truth

The silence hung between us, heavy with unspoken words and shattered dreams. Walker stood before me; a reflection of the pain etched across my own face. His voice, once a source of comfort, now echoed with fragility.

"You can ask me anything," he said, his words carrying the weight of our shared sorrow. There was desperation in his eyes, a plea for understanding, for me to unravel the enigma that had become our shared existence.

For a moment, I opened my mouth, ready to unleash a torrent of anger and confusion. But the words got caught in the tangled mess of emotions inside me. I couldn't find the right words, and the silence became my refuge.

"Then let me explain?" His plea hung in the air like a fragile thread, waiting for me to grasp it. The pain etched on his face mirrored my own, and for a moment, it felt like our worlds were collapsing together.

I nodded, granting him permission to untangle the web of confusion that had enveloped us. A part of me craved answers, while another feared the truth that lay beneath the surface. Walker took a shaky breath, his eyes pleading for me to understand the shards of a story that lay hidden in the recesses of his soul.

I stood there, unable to look Walker in the eyes as he laid bare the fragments of his tragic existence. His words, like shards of glass, pierced through the silence that enveloped us. It was a tale of a stolen childhood, of a life on the run, and the desperate pursuit of a place to belong.

"I was always on the move, finding a place to belong to, and I ended up here. I fell in love with the place and this lake. I once saw you and Harper here, spending the weekend. And I was jealous of how close you guys were, how two people can share moments like this and it's enough."

I clenched my fists, my emotions threatening to overflow. I didn't want to feel sorry for him; I didn't want to empathize with the person who had shattered my world.

"I waited tables, became a gas boy, took part-time jobs at convenience stores and in the library to save money so I could go to school. But one day, I woke up, and my aunt had stolen all the money I saved so she could gamble. I got so pissed, and demanded her to pay me back, but she just slapped me in the face for being so ungrateful. And I knew how much she treasured her booze, so I stole it all, including that car of hers and drove into the night. I drank, and I drove. And then..."

I closed my eyes, the weight of the unspoken truth hanging in the air. I knew what happened next : the tragic collision that claimed my brother's life.

"Why are you here? Why are you back? What are you?" I whispered, my voice tinged with anger and confusion.

"I'm neither here nor there," Walker replied, his words leaving me with more questions than answers.

"Don't give me that. Are you a… ghost? Am I… crazy?"

Reality unraveled itself, revealing the intricate web of illusions I had spun around Walker. The pieces fell into place like a melancholic symphony, harmonizing with the truth I refused to acknowledge. Walker was a ghost—a phantom lingering between realms, tethered to the earthly plane by an unfinished narrative.

Mrs. Cristina's unresponsive gaze when Walker greeted her, the spectral appearance in moments of need, the veiled secrets—all wove into a spectral of truth. Walker was a specter from beyond, a shade intertwined with my existence in ways I had yet to fathom.

As I retraced the footsteps of our supposed shared experiences, the fragments of my own handiwork emerged. The blue tent that sheltered our laughter was a creation inspired by Harper's memory, my hands fumbling with the stakes as I mimicked his motions. The packed dinners, a result of my solitary efforts to mirror the idyllic scenes of companionship.

A surreal epiphany descended upon me: Walker, the presence I had begun to love, was but a whisper in the wind—a ghost caught in the currents of my longing. The encounter by the lake, once perceived as a rescue, was my own struggle for breath, a silent plea to endure for Harper's memory.

The revelation shook the foundation of my perceptions, and a maelstrom of emotions cascaded within. In the twilight between truth and illusion, I grappled with the ethereal presence that had woven itself into the fabric of my reality.

"At first, I didn't understand what I was. But when only you could see me, I understood then."

"Why is it that only I can?" I demanded, my voice growing more desperate.

"Because I need you to forgive me, for what I did. I am terribly sorry, Rory. If only I could—"

"NO, YOU COULDN'T!" I erupted, my anger boiling over. "YOU COULDN'T TURN BACK TIME AND BRING BACK THE BROTHER I LOST. For a year, I blamed myself because I thought it was my fault. And I told you all about it but you said nothing! You, too, made me believe that I was to blame. But no. IT WAS YOU. YOU KILLED HIM. YOU CUT HIS LIFE SHORT."

Walker crumpled before me, sobbing, his own grief laid bare. The weight of my brother's absence pressed upon me like a heavy stone, and my heart echoed with the pain of a thousand shattered pieces.

"I blame you, Walker Louis," I declared, my voice trembling as I uttered his full name. "I can never forgive you."

I turned away, leaving him in the cold waters of the lake, drowning in his own sorrow. My heart continued to break, making it difficult for me to breathe. What had I done to deserve such pain?

18

Mrs. Cristina

I woke up with a lingering heaviness in my heart, the remnants of a dream that felt more like a conversation with the echoes of the past. Harper, in his playful demeanor, asked questions that cut through the tranquil moments we shared by the lake.

"What would you do if I died?" his voice echoed in my mind, a question carrying a weight I hadn't fathomed before.

In the dream, I tossed him a towel, dismissing the question with fervent denial. "Don't talk about things like that!" I scolded him, trying to wrap myself in the illusion of our laughter-filled days.

But Harper persisted, a smile on his face, as if the question were a mere curiosity. "I mean, I want to know that you'd be okay and you'd move on."

I faced him, a determined line on my lips. "I won't be okay," I confessed, a sense of foreboding settling in my chest. "I will mourn for you for years until I grow old."

Harper's expression shifted into a frown; his concern evident. "You shouldn't do that, you know."

"Then you shouldn't die," I retorted, the declaration hanging in the air like an unspoken pact. A promise that we would both grow old, our families remaining close, intertwining through generations. Children, spouses, and grandchildren creating a hundredfold of shared memories.

As the dream dissolved into the reality of waking, the weight on my heart persisted. The dream, a subtle reminder of the unspoken goodbyes that lingered in the corners of my mind.

Days turned into a blur of grief and anger. I sought refuge in Harper's room, the only place that held the remnants of a life shattered by tragedy. On weekdays, I mechanically performed my duties at the library, moving through the motions, avoiding the places that once held shared laughter and warmth with Walker.

Everywhere I looked, Walker was absent, as if he had been erased from existence. Perhaps it was for the best. I told myself, the gnawing void of his absence less painful than the tumultuous emotions his presence ignited.

One Tuesday afternoon, my locker refused to yield to the familiar combination. Seeking a replacement, I approached Mrs. Cristina, who assigned me a new one. To my surprise, as I opened it, remnants of Walker Louis spilled out—fragments of a life cut short.

A worn copy of "Harry Potter and the Half-Blood Prince," an old polo shirt, and a faded ID bearing Walker's unmistakable features lay nestled inside. My heart ached at the sight, tears welling up as I gently caressed his face in the ID photo.

"He was a good kid," Mrs. Cristina offered softly, her presence unnoticed until then.

"Did you know him?" I inquired, struggling to keep my voice steady.

Mrs. Cristina took the ID from my hands, revealing a knowing smile. "I did. He was a lost boy who needed guidance, but he was smart, responsible, and hardworking. He would stay in the library even after his shift just so he could read. I would always find him in the general knowledge section—"

"General knowledge section," I echoed, surprised that Mrs. Cristina was familiar with it too.

She gestured for me to sit beside her on a bench, a silent invitation to share the memories of a boy who had left his traces in the quiet corners of the library. The weight of Walker's absence grew heavier, but within the shared recollections, a connection between us, a bridge between the past and the present, began to form.

As I sat with Mrs. Cristina on the bench, her words unraveling the mysterious threads that bound Walker and me, I couldn't help but feel a mixture of confusion and curiosity.

"I could also see him, you know," Mrs. Cristina said, her voice a gentle revelation that stirred both surprise and intrigue in me.

"You could?" I questioned, my eyes meeting hers in search of an understanding that eluded me.

"Oh, yes. I always believed that lost souls would still wander the earth if there were still words left unsaid, things left undone… And then I saw you smiling at Walker, and I understood. You were his last mission."

Her words hung in the air, sinking into my thoughts. A cascade of memories flooded my mind—the moments Walker had appeared at the lake, the library, and in my life. His presence brought comfort and warmth, filling the void that Harper's absence had left.

"I don't think I'm ready to forgive him yet," I admitted, my gaze dropping to the floor. The complexities of emotions swirled within me, and forgiveness seemed like a distant shore.

"Oh, no, dear," Mrs. Cristina reassured me. "The dead do not need to be forgiven."

Confusion lingered in my eyes as I questioned her meaning, my mind grappling with the profound words she had uttered.

"What do you mean?" I asked, seeking clarity.

Mrs. Cristina's hand gently caressed my face, her touch carrying a wisdom that was beyond age. Her eyes, filled with understanding, met mine.

"I believe you know the answer to that."

Her cryptic response left me contemplating the enigma of Walker's presence and the unspoken connections that bound us, transcending the boundaries of life and death.

19

Family

As I entered the house, the familiar surroundings now carrying a weight of unspoken truths, I found my father waiting for me. His presence, a blend of sorrow and compassion, beckoned me to sit beside him.

"Hi, Dad," I greeted, my voice fragile, reflecting the tumult within.

He smiled, a gesture laden with understanding, and gestured for me to join him. The silence hung heavily between us, a barrier of words waiting to be spoken.

"I'm terribly sorry," my father began, and I instinctively tried to interject, but he stopped me with a gentle wave of his hand. "This was all my fault to begin with."

"Dad, no—" I attempted to defend him, but his words pressed on.

"It's alright, sweetheart. You don't have to protect me."

I kept my gaze lowered, unsure of where this conversation would lead.

"When Tillie and I got married and had Harper, everything felt right in the world. But our marriage was not easy. When

I left town for a business trip, I met this beautiful woman, Rebecca, your mother. We used to go to the same high school, and she was just as lovely as I could remember. I didn't tell her I was married. I was ready to leave Tillie and be with your mother, but when she had you, she wasn't able to make it. Tillie—oh, I couldn't tell you how angry she was. But she didn't want me to leave her. She took you in too. But Harper, he loved you the moment he saw you."

Tears welled in my eyes, and sobs escaped from me as the weight of the revelations bore down.

"Tillie tried her best to be a great mother to you, I saw that. But when we lost Harper, the rage and anger she has harbored over the years for me exploded."

My father took a deep sigh, his own tears mirroring mine.

"I just want you to know that it is me she's angry at. Not you. And give her time. I know you have a special place in her heart."

"You don't know that," I whispered.

"Oh, I know. You remember the time when you and Harper were obsessed with origami?" he asked.

I nodded, still wiping away my tears.

"You made a flower," he continued, "and you gave it to Tillie. She still has it even after all these years. Safely tucked in her purse. That's how I know that you're in her heart."

I couldn't even remember the flower, but it surprised me that my mother still kept it. My father gave me a small hug and kissed my forehead.

"Are you staying tonight?" I asked my father. He nodded with a smile.

I went up to my room, the walls echoing with the weight of the past, but somehow, a glimmer of understanding began to dawn.

The night draped itself over my room, shadows dancing on the walls, and I found solace in the silent company of darkness. I couldn't help but think about the love that had surrounded me as I grew up. I pondered the warmth of a family that embraced me, the laughter shared with Harper, and the comforting presence of parents who tried their best. Imagining a life without that love felt like staring into an abyss, and the thought sent shivers down my spine.

Then, my mind drifted to Walker. A person who, despite growing up devoid of love, radiated kindness and compassion. He wasn't a bad person; he was a person whom the world had dealt a rough hand. The cruelty he experienced from a world that offered little but hardships and tragedy. And, if the world's cruelty wasn't enough, it ended Walker's life in a tragic collision of fate.

My eyes welled up with tears once again as I retrieved Walker's ID from my pocket. I stared at his face, fingers gently caressing the photograph of his curly hair. The guilt gnawed at me, clawing through my chest.

The moment I left Walker alone by the lake, my heart ached with the desire to undo the words I had spoken. To take back the anger, the blame, and the unforgiving stance. If only I could tell him that I forgave him, that it wasn't his fault, and that the cruel twist of fate that entangled him in a car accident was just as tragic as what happened to his brother.

"I'm sorry," I whispered into the void, my voice carried away by the stillness of the night. Holding Walker's ID next to my heart, I wished that somehow, those whispered apologies would reach him, wherever he was.

20

An Old Friend

Waking up to an empty house didn't carry the same weight as it once did. The days at the library continued, still void of Walker's presence, but Mrs. Cristina's newfound warmth offered a small comfort. In the afternoons, I decided to treat myself to a decent meal at a nearby pancake house.

The place was nearly empty when I arrived. Opting for a corner booth, I ordered my favorites—two pieces of chocolate marble pancakes and a vanilla milkshake. As I waited, the sun began its descent, casting warm hues across the sky.

"Hey, Rory," a voice interrupted my thoughts. Looking up, I found Tom, wearing an orange shirt adorned with a pancake in the middle.

"Tom? You work here?" My surprise was evident. He looked different, changed— comely, laid-back, and kind—a far cry from the guy I used to date.

"My mom owns the place," he explained, laying my order in front of me. A small smile graced his face. "I work here every summer."

As he debated whether to leave or stay, Tom settled into the seat across from me. "I was a jerk back then," he admitted. "And I am truly sorry for what I did and what happened to your brother."

I managed a sad smile, thanking him for his words. The sincerity in his eyes was a stark contrast to the person he used to be.

"How have you been?" Tom inquired; sincerity evident in his eyes.

"Feeling better, I guess? I work at the library," I replied.

"That's good. I help out Mrs. Cristina on the weekends." A more genuine smile played on his lips.

I was taken aback. Tom helping at the library was unexpected. "You help at the library?"

"Yeah, I read a lot too. Well, that happened after you left me," he confessed. "I was broken when you left because I really did like you. And I think I still do. But me liking you doesn't justify my previous actions – and again, I'm sorry."

Unexpected confessions spilled from Tom, and I listened, absorbing the changes in him. "So yeah, when I heard that your brother died, I wanted to go to you, but my mom thought it wouldn't be for the best. She found out what I did, and I got more than an earful. So, I spent the day reading because it was the only way I thought would make me feel close to you, and then it became a hobby. I know you love Harry Potter, so I started with that."

A small laugh escaped me at the irony. "Well, all I can say is that I'm happy you found solace in reading."

"I sure did," Tom replied. "I just started Hunger Games."

My eyes widened in fascination. "Another one of my favorites."

"Sorry, you should be eating. The pancakes are really good." Tom stood up, giving me one last look. "Guess I'll see you around?"

I nodded. "Sure." As he left, I pondered the unpredictability of change and the unexpected apologies life could offer.

21

This Love

The days blended together as I stopped by the lake every time my shift at the library concluded, hoping to catch a glimpse of Walker. The emptiness lingered, and the lake seemed to lose its luster without him. The usual sparkle was replaced with a dullness that mirrored my own emotions.

One Sunday, unable to shake the persistent thoughts of Walker, I ventured to the lake once more. The usual solitude felt heavier, and I couldn't help but call out his name, hoping for a response.

"Walker! Walker!" My voice echoed across the desolate landscape, but there was no sign of him. The familiar sights seemed muted, the forest, once vibrant, now felt eerily lonely.

Defeated, I sank to the ground. Tears welled up as I faced the reality of missing Walker. It was a longing that went beyond companionship; it was a connection that went beyond the boundaries of life and death.

"Rory?"

His voice echoed, and I turned around, hope flickering back to life. There he was— Walker. His beautiful face, his distinctive curls—he looked just as I remembered. Without a second thought, I rushed towards him, yearning for the warmth of his embrace.

But as I reached out, something strange happened. I went straight through him, like a phantom passing through the air. Confusion painted my face as I stumbled backward, my hands trembling.

"Walker?" I whispered, a mix of disbelief and desperation in my voice. He stood before me, unchanged and seemingly real, yet my touch couldn't reach him. The truth dawned on me—Walker was no longer a tangible part of my world. He existed in the echoes of the lake, in the memories we shared, forever etched into the fabric of my heart.

The air around us felt charged with an otherworldly energy. Walker's form remained before me, but a growing translucence now adorned him, like the ethereal mist that hung above the lake at dawn. Confusion clawed at my mind; I had touched him before, held him close, and now, my outstretched hands grasped only the chill of the evening air.

His smile persisted; a gentle reassurance painted on his fading face.

"Rory," he began, his voice carrying a whisper of melancholy, "things change. I don't entirely understand why or how, but it's happening."

I struggled to find words, my voice a mere tremor. "But… we were fine before. I could touch you. We held hands, we kissed!"

Walker's eyes held a depth of understanding, a wisdom that transcended the boundary between our worlds. "It's complicated. Maybe my time here is coming to an end, or perhaps it's because you're starting to move forward. The lake brought us together, but it's not where you belong forever."

The lake whispered its secrets, as if mourning the imminent departure of a bond forged in the quiet depths. I clung to the fragments of Walker's fading figure, desperate to hold onto the connection that had grown so profound.

"But I love you," I confessed, the words surprising even myself. In that moment, they were the purest truth I could utter.

Pain etched Walker's features, mirroring the depths of his own emotions. His sobs cut through the silence, a symphony of shared grief. "I think I loved you the moment I saw you, Rory. And I love you more even now."

As he inched forward, Walker's lips met my forehead. In that brief touch, a cascade of memories flooded my senses, moments etched in the fabric of our shared existence.

There was laughter by the lake, where Walker first laid eyes on me, chasing me alongside Harper. The library encounters, hidden behind shelves, watching the sparkle in my eyes as I returned a book. The quiet afternoons spent reading Harry Potter, our shared love for the magical world binding us closer.

The final memory, etched in the sterile halls of the hospital, revealed the fragile threads connecting our lives. Walker, wheeled into the emergency room, glimpsing me through the haze, his heart aching with a love that surpassed the tangible.

The weight of realization pressed down on me. Walker wasn't just an apparition, a figment of my grieving heart. He was a soul, a presence that had seeped into the very essence of my existence. Now, he stood at the precipice of departure, his purpose fulfilled.

"You have to let go, Rory," Walker whispered, his voice a fragile echo. "Let go of the guilt, the blame. You deserve happiness, free from the chains of the past. You have to let me go."

Tears streamed down my face as I grappled with the agony of parting. "But I need you."

Walker's gaze held a bittersweet tenderness. "You don't need me, Rory. You have the strength within you. Find forgiveness within your own heart. It's time."

The sun bathed the world in a radiant glow, its warmth a cruel contrast to the cold ache that gripped my heart. As Walker's form waned, he glanced upward, captivated by the brilliance above.

"What a great day to feel alive," he said, his words lingering in the air like a gentle breeze. I couldn't bear to tear my eyes away from the fading figure before me.

"You gave me life in my last moments, Rory," Walker continued, his hand outstretched. I reached out instinctively, yearning for a touch that would never grace my senses again. "Now, live your life to the fullest."

"No, I can't. I need you," I pleaded, my voice breaking under the weight of sorrow. "I can't lose you too."

Walker's tone, though tinged with sadness, held a comforting assurance. "Sshh, you're all good now. You will travel the world like you wanted. You'll work at the library, be a writer even! You'll spend weekends working in charity–"

"But you can come with me," I insisted, desperation seeping into my words.

"You know that's not possible," Walker replied, his expression more mournful. "Now, you have to let me go. Turn your back on me and keep moving forward. Don't look back, Rory. Just keep walking."

"I can't… I can't do that," I protested, my knees trembling.

"You can. It's time to move on," he urged.

With a heavy heart, I took one last, lingering look at Walker's beautiful face. I turned around, my sobs echoing through the emptiness of the forest.

"No matter what happens, don't look back. No matter what you hear, don't look back," Walker's voice lingered, a comforting echo in my ears.

"I love you, Rory. Now, go."

Every step felt like a betrayal, tearing at my soul.

Laughter filled the forest—Walker's voice calling to me, urging me to return, to dive into the water with him. The tire swing awaited our shared joy. But I forced myself forward, the weight of his words echoing in my heart.

I have to let him go.

"Don't look back," I whispered through the tears, a mantra to guide me on the unseen path ahead. "Don't look back."

22

Life and Death

The path led me to Mrs. Cristina's doorstep, a haven of solace in my time of need. It was a revelation that came to me during the night I studied Walker's ID, where I discovered Mrs. Cristina's name as his emergency contact.

Her eyes, wise and comforting, acknowledged the turmoil that had overtaken my spirit. Without uttering a word, she pulled me into an embrace that felt like the warmest of sanctuaries.

"Oh, my dear, come here," she whispered, guiding me gently inside.

Mrs. Cristina's home was a testament to the warmth within. Books adorned the walls, and plates of vibrant hues adorned her shelves. Coffee mugs, each with its unique story, hung gracefully in her kitchen. She poured hot cocoa into one such mug and handed it to me, a gesture of solace in a moment of despair.

As the tears continued to stream down my face, Mrs. Cristina reached out and held my hand. "Tell me what happened, dear."

I recounted every detail, from the first moment Walker

appeared in my life to the heart-wrenching farewell at the lake. Mrs. Cristina listened intently, her eyes reflecting the depth of her understanding.

When the last words escaped my lips, she offered a serene smile before speaking, "You saved him."

Confusion marked my face, prompting Mrs. Cristina to unravel the intricacies of Walker's journey.

"Not all wandering souls find their way to the afterlife, Rory. Some linger, unable to see the light. But you, my dear, you helped Walker in ways beyond your comprehension."

"How?" I asked, my voice laden with curiosity. "I believe he was the one who saved me."

Mrs. Cristina's gentle laughter filled the room. "You saved each other. Walker grew up in a world devoid of love, yearning for a place to belong. He longed for friendship, companionship, and you provided all that. To him, you were more than enough. Your love for him became the beacon that guided him across."

A cascade of sobs escaped me, but beneath the sorrow, a newfound understanding blossomed. Walker, my ethereal companion, was on a journey to a place where peace awaited him. My love, though unable to keep him in my grasp, had been the bridge to a realm of tranquility beyond.

A gentle lull took me into slumber on Mrs. Cristina's couch. As I stirred from my rest, the moonlit night revealed itself through the windows. The warmth of the setting sun had long faded, replaced by a calm, quiet darkness. However, I wasn't alone.

In the soft glow emanating from the kitchen, I caught the murmur of voices. My father's kind and familiar tones mingled with Mrs. Cristina's wisdom, weaving a conversation I wasn't meant to hear. With careful steps, I approached the source of their hushed deliberations.

"You think it would be good for her?" My father's words held a note of concern, and my curiosity piqued. What were they discussing about me?

"You just have to support her, give her options, and allow her to decide." Mrs. Cristina's advice floated in the air, and I wondered what decisions lay ahead.

Sensing my presence, they turned toward me, their expressions a mixture of warmth and worry. "I called Simon to pick you up," Mrs. Cristina explained. "But if you'd like to stay here for the night, it's fine too."

Gratitude welled up within me, and I embraced Mrs. Cristina, whispering my thanks into her ear. With a lingering hug, I bid her goodnight and joined my father for the ride home.

The car moved through the quiet night, the hum of the engine the only sound between us. Thoughts of Walker swirled in my mind, his face and voice still vivid in my memory. The unexpected turns that summer had taken left me grappling with emotions I never anticipated.

Upon arriving home, the silence persisted. My father's gaze lingered on the road ahead, allowing me the space to navigate the storm within. Summer's enchanting promises had morphed into a bittersweet journey, leaving me with echoes of laughter and the ghostly whispers of a love that surpassed the boundaries of life and death.

23

Goodbye, Walker

The air hung heavy with the weight of summer's last breaths. A week had passed since I let Walker go. The lake seemed to mourn his absence, its ripples whispering secrets only he and I once knew.

With trembling hands, I clutched a letter—my farewell, an ethereal message to a specter who had become my confidant in the shadows. Tears blurred the ink as I unfolded the parchment, whispering my words aloud as if they could traverse the boundary between worlds.

"Walker,

In the hush of the dwindling summer, I find myself compelled to write my gratitude into the wind. This wondrous season, entwined with the threads of your spectral presence, bore witness to the magic you infused into my life.

You were my hope within reach, an angel navigating the corridors between realms. In the quiet of the forest, you painted moments of beauty with strokes of laughter and companionship. With you, life exceeded the mundane; you were everything good in the world.

As the sun sets on our summer, I realize you were the gentle push I needed to step into the future with newfound courage. Your touch, though intangible, lingers as a beacon guiding me towards dreams, I once thought unattainable.

In your absence, I promise to carry the echoes of our shared laughter, the warmth of your invisible presence, and the love that blossomed within my heart. You were more than a ghost; you were the guardian of memories that would inspire me to live a good life.

Walker, as the seasons change, my love for you remains eternal.

With all my heart,
Rory"

As the final words of my letter to Walker lingered in the air, a gentle breeze swept through the forest, enveloping me in its ephemeral caress. It was as if the very breath of the lake carried my words to the ether.

The rustling leaves whispered secrets of a spectral presence, and in that moment, I felt Walker's essence all around me. He wasn't just a memory; he was the wind that tousled my hair, the echo in the rustling leaves, and the soft ripple across the lake's surface. Walker was the intangible force that animated the very heart of the forest, and, in turn, my own.

I closed my eyes, allowing the breeze to play with the edges of my letter, a silent acknowledgment that my words had found their way to him. The lake, once a haven introduced to me by Harper, had transformed into a sanctuary of memories, each ripple and gust echoing the presence of those who had left an indelible mark on its shores.

Harper, who unveiled the magic of this place, and Walker, who infused it with enchantment. Together, they had become the guardians of this sacred space—brothers in spirit.

The lake's surface shimmered with the fading sunlight, a reflection of the celestial bond that transcended the veil between worlds. In that tranquil moment, I felt a profound connection, not just to the lake but to the ethereal thread that bound us all together.

"Thank you," I murmured to the unseen, to Walker, to the essence that infused the very air around me.

With a heart both heavy and uplifted, I turned away from the lake, knowing that the echoes of this summer would guide me through the seasons to come.

24

The Next Chapter

"Ladies and gentlemen, esteemed faculty, proud parents, and my fellow graduates, today marks the culmination of years of hard work, resilience, and determination. I'm Rory Grant. As the Editor-in-Chief of our school's paper and the President of the Book Club, it's an honor to stand before you. In these pages and discussions, we've woven narratives that reflect the essence of our diverse journeys. Life is a huge blanket of stories, each thread unique and precious. It is crucial to believe in ourselves, recognizing that our voices matter, and our stories are worth sharing. Amidst the chaos of deadlines and the whirlwind of assignments, let us not forget to savor the small moments—the laughter, the camaraderie, and the shared passion for literature. In the pursuit of success, it's easy to drown in misery. But let us not be defined by our challenges; let us be shaped by our ability to overcome them. Graduation is not an endpoint; it's a new beginning. As we step into the world beyond these familiar walls, let us carry a newfound sense of hope. Let us embrace change, for it is the harbinger of growth and opportunity. Congratulations, my fellow graduates. Our stories have only just begun, and the pages ahead are blank, waiting for us to pen the tales of our lives. Here's to believing in ourselves, appreciating life's little wonders, and moving forward with unwavering hope. Thank you."

Graduation day arrived, marking the end of a significant chapter in my life and the beginning of a new one. My father was there, standing proudly amidst the crowd, capturing moments with the camera that had been a constant companion throughout our journey. Mrs. Cristina, with her wise and kind eyes, stood beside him, offering silent support.

My mother's absence lingered, but I didn't harbor any bitterness. Loss taught me to understand the depths of grief, and I respected her need for solitude in facing the echoes of the past.

Photographs were snapshots of joy, capturing the elation of friendships forged during my time in the book club. We exchanged promises of keeping in touch, but the unpredictability of life loomed ahead. Tom, who had transformed into a different person over the years, graduated as well. We posed for a picture together, acknowledging the shared history that shaped us.

Amidst the cheerful chaos, Mrs. Cristina handed me a gift, a beautifully adorned edition of Frances Hodgson Burnett's "The Secret Garden." It was a classic, filled with magic and nostalgia.

"I want you to have it," she said, and I hugged her with gratitude. The library had become a haven for me, a place where Walker's presence lingered, and Mrs. Cristina and I forged an unbreakable bond. "We're going to miss you at the library," Mrs. Cristina expressed, and I nodded in understanding. The library, a place of solace and connection, had been a constant in my life.

Graduations were about endings and beginnings. The ceremony marked the conclusion of one adventure and the threshold of another. I had chosen to pursue a Bachelor's degree in Library and Information Science, fueled by a desire to become a chief librarian someday. My father supported this decision wholeheartedly, recognizing the passion that blossomed within me.

As I stood on the precipice of the future, I felt the echoes of that summer. The love, the loss, and the lessons had shaped me into someone ready to embrace the world. The next chapter awaited, and I was determined to fill its pages with stories of resilience, love, and the magic that lingered in unexpected places.

The End

25

Bonus: Walker's POV

The convenience store's sliding glass doors chimed as I stepped out into the cool morning air. The graveyard shift had just ended. I worked at the 24/7 convenience store down the road, a mundane routine that offered a distraction from the chaotic reality that was my life.

Deciding I didn't want to face the turmoil of my aunt's house just yet, I found myself drawn to the forest. The stone path led me to a hidden gem, a beautiful lake surrounded by nature's embrace.

Hesitant footsteps guided me to the edge of the clearing, where laughter danced through the air. Behind a large tree, I stole glances at the source of this joy.

There, amidst the serene beauty of the lake, was a young boy and girl, siblings by the look of it. The boy was chasing her with algae in hand, their laughter creating a symphony that echoed through the trees.

"Stop it, Harper! So annoying. You're the worst brother ever!" the girl exclaimed, her giggles punctuating her words. The sun's rays painted her face in a warm glow, revealing a breathtaking beauty that captivated me. Her eyes sparkled like stars, and her black hair danced with the wind.

As I stood there, an invisible spectator to their shared moments, a strange feeling washed over me. A mix of awe at the beauty before me and a pang of jealousy for the bond they shared. In each other, they found a home that would last an eternity. I yearned for something similar, a connection that had eluded me.

"Rory!" the boy, Harper, called out, hanging from a tire swing. "Come, you have to try this!"

Rory, as beautiful as her name, shook her head, her laughter ringing in the air. "I would never get on that swing."

"Come on, you're missing out!"

She stuck her tongue out playfully, and the sound of her laughter lingered like a sweet melody. It made me laugh too, a rare occurrence in my solitary existence.

"I'd rather read my book in peace," Rory retorted, her playful glare adding to the enchantment. The moment she dove into the pages, captivated by the world within, I found myself entranced.

"So, she's a reader too," I whispered to myself, feeling a subtle flutter in my chest.

As I left the lake that day, I couldn't shake off the image of her face from my mind. I pondered on ways to introduce myself, wondering what she liked, what she was into. I couldn't get the sight of her pretty face out of my head.

I entered the small, rundown house that I reluctantly called home. Exhaustion weighed heavily on my shoulders; a product of the graveyard shifts at the convenience store. My body craved rest, but my mind buzzed with memories of the lake, the tire swing, and Rory's laughter that echoed in my ears.

The front door creaked as I closed it behind me, but my escape from the reality of my aunt's house was short-lived. A stinging slap landed on the back of my head, jolting me back to the harshness of my surroundings.

"What took you so long?" My aunt's voice slurred with alcohol and anger.

"I went out for a walk," I replied, my expression a mask hiding the emotions bubbling within.

"Out rambling when you should be cooking me breakfast? You're useless," she spat, her words stinging as much as the impact of her hand.

The house reeked of liquor and cigars, a toxic blend that assaulted my senses. It was a familiar scene, a chaotic mess that mirrored the tumult within our home. Without a glance back, I walked past my aunt, her angry words fading into the background. Her calls were mere echoes in the corridors of my mind as I sought refuge in the solitude of my room.

Closing the door behind me, I allowed the small room to swallow the tiredness that clung to my bones. The memories of the lake, of Rory's enchanting presence, became a lifeline in the sea of chaos that was my reality. It gave me a glimpse of something different, something beautiful, and I clung to it as I lay on my tattered bed.

The soft rustle of the leaves by the lake and the distant laughter played in my mind, drowning out the harshness of my aunt's angry tirade. In the sanctuary of my room, I closed my eyes, hoping that sleep would bring with it dreams of a world where the tire swing swung freely, and Rory's smile lit up the darkest corners of my thoughts.

The day stretched endlessly before me, each passing hour marked by the dull throb of hunger gnawing at my insides. I lay on my bed, the worn-out mattress providing meager comfort. Sleep became my refuge, a temporary escape from the harsh reality that awaited me outside the confines of my room.

Ignoring the persistent growl in my belly, I succumbed to the sweet embrace of slumber. Dreams offered solace, transporting me to a place where the lake sparkled, and laughter echoed through the rustling leaves. In that realm, hunger was forgotten, replaced by the warmth of memories.

It was six in the evening when I finally stirred, as if the shadows had granted me a reprieve. The dim glow of twilight seeped through the cracks in the curtains. Hunger had become a constant companion, yet I found myself yearning for something beyond the physical ache in my stomach.

Cautiously, I crawled out of the window, my movements silent as I maneuvered through the familiar escape route. The air outside embraced me, carrying the scent of the impending night. The journey to the convenience store was habitual, a routine etched into the fabric of my existence.

As I approached the store, a fleeting hope crossed my mind—that tonight would be one of those rare, empty nights. A night when I could lose myself in the world of words, the realm crafted by the pages of the book nestled in my bag.

The bell above the door jingled as I entered, the familiar chime a signal that marked my entrance into a space that offered more than just necessities. My eyes darted around, surveying the solitude that enveloped the store. A sigh of relief escaped me, and I made my way to the dimly lit corner.

The tattered seat welcomed me, and I retrieved the book from my bag, its cover worn but its pages brimming with untold adventures. The first sentence transported me to a world far removed from my own, a world where hunger and hardship were mere echoes in the background.

The dull hum of the convenience store's fluorescent lights flickered as the clock inched towards nine in the evening. The silence of the night was only interrupted by the soft buzzing of the freezer, and I couldn't help but feel the heaviness of solitude.

As I half-heartedly arranged bottles by the counter, the bell above the entrance chimed—a sound that rarely brought excitement during the late shift. But then, there she was, illuminated by the store's sterile lights, standing by the ice cream section.

"Oops," she chuckled, her voice like a familiar melody. I knocked over a few water bottles in my orchestrated clumsiness. The noise gave me away, and her gaze locked onto mine.

"Luckily, you weren't hit on the head!" she quipped, bending down to help me gather the fallen bottles. My eyes were drawn to her every movement, and for a moment, I forgot how to breathe.

"Vanilla or mint chocolate?" she asked, unexpectedly breaking the silence. I stammered, caught off guard by the abrupt question. Her laughter rang in my ears, a sound I had missed more than I realized.

She shrugged playfully. "Both it is."

At the counter, her genuine smile sent my heart into a frenzy. As she paid, I anticipated her departure, but instead, she handed me the vanilla ice cream. My hand, unaccustomed to such warmth, received the cold treat, and I was left flustered.

"You look pale. Thought you needed a bit of sugar," she said, her kindness wrapping around me like a gentle embrace. With a final smile and a casual "bye," she left, leaving me stunned and grateful for the unexpected encounter.

As the bell chimed once more, signaling her departure, I

stood there, vanilla ice cream in hand, and realized that life's surprises could be sweet—a stark contrast to the monotony of my existence. I tasted the cold sweetness, savoring not just the ice cream but the warmth she left behind.

In that quiet convenience store, I found a glimmer of hope, and as I devoured the vanilla treat, I couldn't help but agree with the unspoken sentiment: what a beautiful day to be alive.

About the Author

Joline Lim is a well-caffeinated 27-year-old accountant by day and wordsmith by night. She calls the Queen City of the South, Cebu, her home. A dedicated reader and a fervent Harry Potter enthusiast, Joline finds solace in the enchanting world of literature. Her passion for both numbers and narratives creates a harmonious blend in her life where each day unfolds with a perfect balance of logic and imagination.

You can connect with me on:
- https://www.beacons.ai/thejoediary
- https://www.instagram.com/thejoediary